# THE BRATS

# The Brats

*To George,
Best wishes from
Tony Paul          16-11-04*

### TONY PAUL

Woodfield Publishing

First edition, published in 2002 by

WOODFIELD PUBLISHING
Woodfield House, Babsham Lane, Bognor Regis
West Sussex PO21 5EL, England.

© Tony Paul, 2002

All rights reserved.
No part of this publication may be reproduced
or transmitted in any form or by any means,
electronic or mechanical, nor may it be stored
in any information storage and retrieval system,
without prior permission from the publisher.

The right of Tony Paul
to be identified as Author of this work
has been asserted by him in accordance with
the Copyright, Designs and Patents Act 1988

ISBN 1-903953-26-X

## Contents

1. Ends and Beginnings ............................................................. 1
2. In Greenock ........................................................................... 8
3. Leaving home ...................................................................... 15
4. At the dockside ................................................................... 21
5. The voyage begins .............................................................. 29
6. The stowaways meet the Captain and Mate ..................... 40
7. The hardships begin ........................................................... 49
8. Bryson seeks revenge ......................................................... 60
9. John gets a coat – and a haircut ........................................ 69
10. Prelude to a storm ............................................................... 77
11. The cold bites ...................................................................... 90
12. Bryson in trouble ................................................................ 95
13. Snowballs ........................................................................... 106
14. Hughie gets a beating ....................................................... 113
15. A bad night ........................................................................ 122
16. Bryson finds a meal and regrets it ................................... 131
17. Bryson takes a beating ...................................................... 139
18. The Captains meet ............................................................ 148
19. Currie finds a thief ............................................................ 159
20. Chains, a meal and a wash ............................................... 169

| | | |
|---|---|---|
| 21. | Into the ice | 180 |
| 22. | More ice | 192 |
| 23. | Another beating | 205 |
| 24. | Sent ashore | 216 |
| 25. | The long walk | 225 |
| 26. | The ice claims its victims | 235 |
| 27. | The ordeal ends | 245 |
| Epilogue | | 257 |

## *Introduction*

In the mid 1970s my parents were holidaying in Scotland and on their way back they went to Greenock to visit some relatives that they hadn't seen for thirty years or more. While there they were told briefly of the adventures of my great grandfather who, as a boy of twelve, stowed away to Canada. My mother was intrigued by the story and learned that this voyage was the subject of a chapter in John Donald's book on stowaways, a copy of which was in The Watt Library. She read the story and was so taken with it that she went to a local newsagents, bought a pad of Basildon Bond and copied it out word for word. Upon my mother's death my father was sorting through her papers and found this account, which he then gave to me.

I became interested and began further exploration of the story. My researches took me to Greenock, Edinburgh and Newfoundland. Using as a basis the precognition evidence produced prior to the trial of the Captain and Mate of the Arran, I pieced the story together, carefully filling in the holes in this 'net curtain' of fact, to create a story that is both accurate and evocative of the voyage and its time. I dedicate this book to my Mother who would have been very proud and pleased to see this story brought into the light.

## About the Author

Following two former careers – the first as a musician and songwriter in a rock band in the 1960s and the second in the Fire Service, where he rose to the rank of Station Officer – he is now a professional artist and art tutor, working both in adult education and on residential courses. He writes two monthly columns for the magazine *Leisure Painter*, has shown work in the Royal Academy Summer Exhibition and is a colour adviser to Daler-Rowney, the art materials manufacturer.

He has always had an interest in writing and a previous book, 'The Story of the Fire Service' was published by Almark in 1975. He has also had short stories published in popular magazines.

Tony Paul was born in Poole and now lives in Bournemouth with his wife, two of his four daughters and Molly the Labrador.

## Acknowledgements

I would like to express my grateful thanks to the following people and organisations for their help in the research for this book. Ian Burton for all his advice throughout the writing of the book. Gerry Byrne for his careful Internet searches on my behalf. Peter Coles of the Wessex Newfoundland Society, Poole. Mrs Lesley Couperwhite of The Watt Library, Greenock, a remarkably conscientious and thorough researcher on my behalf, Paul Sturm of the Public Record Office at Kew. General Register Office for Scotland, Edinburgh. Catherine Power of the Newfoundland Historical Society, St John's Newfoundland. The Memorial University of Newfoundland, St John's Newfoundland.

While I have been careful to use the real names of the characters involved in this story, I had a problem because two of the stowaways, McGinnes & McEwan, shared the same Christian name – Hugh. As this could result in confusion, particularly in the dialogue, for the sake of clarity I have changed Hugh McGinnes's Christian name to Jimmy. I hope that readers will forgive this small departure from reality.

# 1. Ends and Beginnings

The shock of hitting the ice brought him to his senses. He could not understand why he had fallen down. Trying to move, he could sense his clothes being gripped, as they froze to the ice. What little feeling remained in his body was being drawn downwards.

When he had last fallen it had hurt like hell; twelve-year-old flesh was no match for ice as hard as granite. Why, he wondered, did he feel no pain? He wanted to cry, he had cried the last time he had fallen, but then it had hurt. He groaned involuntarily.

"Johnny!" The voice was Bryson's.

John pulled his hair free of the ice and looked up at the youth, on a floe some yards away. He was standing stiffly upright, like a statue against the evening light, with his hands outstretched, as if balancing.

"Johnny!" His voice was more urgent now. John tried to answer but the words were too difficult to form. There was panic in Bryson's voice.

"Johnny, for the love of Christ, answer will ye!"

Again John tried to respond. He could numbly feel his mouth opening but nothing came out.

Bryson began to sob: "Johnny, are ye there? Please ... tell me ye's there ... I cannae see. I'm blind. I canna see nothin'.

Where are ye Johnny?" His voice trailed off into sobs. "I canna see... Help me!" screamed Bryson, "Help me ... Someone..." His voice was lost in the emptiness of the ice field. Now he pleaded, "Please God, if ye exist, help me." John lay and watched Bryson hunch his body, cry lustily, and cover his face with his hands. The effort of looking at Bryson proved too much and he closed his eyes. He was tired, so very tired.

'So this is how I die,' he thought, 'after all I've been through'. He felt strangely detached. 'If this is death, it's nae so bad.' His mind was floating, free of pain, at peace. Bryson's sobs had become distant echoes. John opened his eyes but could not focus on the youth. He could feel himself drifting away and fancied that he could smell the tannery near the railway in Greenock.

"Johnny!" The voice wasn't Bryson's.

'Hughie!' he thought. 'It's Hughie!'

The boy skidded on the cobbles as he came up to John. He was out of breath.

"I was just goin' round tae your place. It's a wonder that I saw ye in this fog."

"What ye doin' in Greenock?"

"I'm on an errand for my Ma." He held up a burlap bag. "Got tae deliver it tae me Auntie. I've tae go back tae Glasgow tomorrow."

"It's as well I saw ye today. I shan't be here this time tomorrow."

"Where ye goin' then?"

John smiled. "I'm stowin' awa'. There's a smart ship called the Arran, leaves for Quebec tomorrow. I'm stowin awa' wi' Jamie an' Robbie from school – it's all arranged."

"Can I come?"

John looked doubtful.

"Och, go on…" said Hughie. "I'd rather come wi' ye than go back tae rotten Glasgow! It'll be a great adventure."

John softened. "I'm happy for ye tae come, but I dinna ken what Jamie'll say."

"Och he won't mind, I get on wi' Jamie and Robbie."

"Tell ye what," said John, as the fruit and veg stall came into view, "I want tae get an apple for Rosie."

"I wouldnae mind one either," said Hughie.

"I'll get three then. One for each of us. You can be the stoolie."

Hughie frowned. "I'm always the stoolie. Why can't you be the stoolie for a change?"

John rattled the stick he was holding against the railings as they walked along. "You're a much better stoolie than me, always have been. You're the best stoolie in the world." The stick broke and John tossed it over the fence.

"You're just sayin' that cause you don't want tae do it."

"No I'm not," said John lightly, "I mean it."

Hughie allowed himself a small, private smile. "Alright then, what ship shall I say?"

"Say the Arran"

"Isn't that our ship'?"

"Aye"

Hughie drew away from John and, with an anxiety he hoped wouldn't show, approached the stallholder.

"Excuse me sir, I've just come from Glasgow. I've tae meet my uncle on a ship called the Arran. Can ye tell me where she's berthed?"

The large man looked along the dockside, removed his cap and scratched his head.

"Arran?" he said to himself. "Arran... I think it's in Victoria Harbour."

Hughie positioned himself so that the man turned his back on the stall, at which point John approached.

"How do I get there?" asked the boy with wide-eyed innocence.

"Well, you could see it from here if it weren't for the fog," he began, as John took three apples from the box on display behind him. "... just keep on along this road and it's the first harbour ye come to."

"Thank ye, Sir." Hughie touched the peak of his cap in respect and turned to go. His arm was grabbed by the stallholder. The boy froze momentarily. As he turned to face his captor he noticed John sauntering nonchalantly away from the stall, his jacket pockets bulging.

"Aye Sir?" Hughie's voice betrayed the fear he felt. The stallholder let go and Hughie ran off, his hobnail boots sparking on the cobbles.

"Funny boy," murmured the stallholder, scratching his head, "I was only going to gi' you an apple…"

The frightened boy ran past John who, thinking they had been found out, also broke into a run. Hughie skidded around the first corner and stopped, panting, his back against the wall. John followed him into the alley.

"Bastard!" said Hughie.

"Wha's up wi' you?" panted John.

"Wha's up wi' me? I nearly had a heart attack … grabbed me he did … I thought the game was up … I'm not bein' stoolie next time."

John took a green apple from his pocket and gave it to his friend. "Worth it for a nice apple ain't it?"

Hughie looked at the shiny fruit as if weighing its value. "S'pose so" he said and took a bite, which he spat out a second later.

"Wha's the matter now?" John asked.

"It's a bloody cooker, sour as a lemon!"

"Well, if you're goin' tae be fussy…"

Hughie dropped it to the ground and kicked it hard. "Goal!" he shouted, throwing his arms into the air, as it bounced over the quayside cobbles and disappeared into the fog.

Despite being the younger, at eleven, Hughie was taller than John, but thinner, with a delicate look about him. In addition to a shabby grey suit and tie he wore a peaked cap, which had earflaps tied up over the crown. Both his cap and his hobnail boots appeared too big for him.

John was typical of the children who lived in the overcrowded tenement blocks in Greenock. They all seemed to be made from the grey/dun of the town itself. His jacket was of an indeterminate colour, frayed at the elbows and cuffs, and a grubby white shirt and choker could be seen above its high-buttoned lapels. His trousers were shapeless, faded and worn and, below the tattered hems were thin calves and grey stained feet, which, where washed by puddles, revealed pink toes.

The mousy mop of hair, which protruded from beneath a worn cap, was spangled like a dewy cobweb with droplets of water. Beneath this wayward thatch was a damp face, flushed with robust health. Although not a handsome boy, there was a look in his eyes that expressed an open character and an enthusiasm for life.

They walked together to the corner of East Quay Lane and stopped.

"See ye tomorrow," said Hughie. "I've my errand tae run first but I'll be wi' ye as soon as I can."

He turned up the lane and John continued along East Breast. He began eating one of his apples but, after a couple of mouthfuls, grimaced and tossed it out into the harbour. As he passed the dry dock he saw a cart turning into Long Vennel. He quickened his pace and called out to the driver.

"Mr Hobbs, Mr Hobbs!" The driver turned around, reined in the horse and peered through the gloom to see who was calling so urgently. He smiled when he saw the boy.

"Johnnie Paul… How are ye laddie? Jump up with me, I'll gi' ye a ride to the corner – I take it ye're goin' home?"

"Aye," said John, breathlessly, "Thank ye sir."

"Its a long time past school. Kept in for bein' naughty were ye?" asked Hobbs, as he stirred the horse into action with a flick of the reins.

"No!" chuckled the boy. "I've been watchin' the ships unloadin'. Have you seen em' queuein' outside the harbours. I've never seen it so busy. Ye can hardly get along the quay for timber."

"Aye, its a busy time now," said the driver earnestly, "there's money to be made, and thank God for it."

The tenement buildings at the junction of Long Vennel and Dalrymple Street faded into the brownish fog that hung over the town. Each chill droplet of moisture in the air was tainted with the stink of industrial Greenock. The tanneries, the foundries and the flesh market, the sugar refineries, slaughterhouses, soap and candle factories, the breweries and the docks added to the stench of the town's own streets and closes, to give the air an almost stifling density.

Despite the cold, dark inhospitality of the early April afternoon the streets were busy and people, wagons and carts moved in and out of the fog like noisy spectres. From Dalrymple Street the cart could be heard climbing Long Vennel. It was not visible but the sound of its metal tyred wheels on the cobbles echoed sharply from the tall tenements which lined the narrow street.

As it appeared like a vague, ragged shadow from the fog, it stopped and John jumped down from the vehicle. He thanked the driver and, hunched against the cold, trotted off, barefooted, along Dalrymple Street towards the Town Hall.

## 2. In Greenock

Number eleven Dalrymple Street stood, dark and stern-featured, alongside the town hall. It formed the left flank of the cobbled courtyard; its dour, plain facade in contrast to that of the classically decorated municipal building. On this April afternoon, the town hall was barely visible behind its screen of fog, which made the tenement appear more prominent and foreboding than usual.

The ground floor of the four storey building that fronted the street was occupied by cordage wholesalers, whose fascia sign in tarnished gold lettering gave slight relief to the grubby, black-painted woodwork framing the windows and doors.

The shop window featured a fly-blown display of the cordage which the wholesaler stocked. To the left of this unimpressive display was an arched opening that gave access to Buchanan's Close, a narrow alley which served a range of decrepit buildings tacked on to the rear of the dour tenement. This close was one of the most notorious areas of Greenock. Among the honest poor who lived in the crumbling slum dwellings, was a motley assembly of thugs, petty criminals, drunks, prostitutes and their pimps.

John, still trotting, emerged from the fog. He turned and skipped lightly down the alley, weaving around the puddles as he went. In a recess between two of the ramshackle buildings was an area crudely fenced off and with a timber lean to structure in one corner. The ground inside the enclosure was a quagmire of foul smelling mud. John walked over to it. "Rosie." he called. From the lean to a grey muddied pig emerged and trotted over to greet him. "Hello Rosie. I've somethin' for ye." He took the apple from his pocket.

The pig nudged him, snatched the meal he offered and crunched it noisily, uttering appreciative grunts. John stroked the coarse bristle of Rosie's muddy head and ears, earning further grunts of satisfaction.

Having finished her apple the pig pushed her head through a gap in the fence and nuzzled at John's pocket, smearing stinking mud across his jacket. "I've nae more for ye. It's nae guid keepin' on. Look, you're gettin' me messy. Away wi' ye Rosie!"

John ducked away from the pig, crossed a small yard, past a dung heap and a wittering drunk and skipped up the three granite steps to the decaying sandstone building where he lived. The small entrance hallway was dimly lit. As he approached the stair, more by touch than vision in the murk, he was aware of a rhythmic rustling and breathing coming from the dark spandrel of the staircase. Choosing to ignore this familiar sound, he started up the stair. "She'll murder me. I'm covered," he muttered, brushing his muddy jacket with his hand.

He had almost reached the first landing when a voice came from below.

"Is that you Johnnie?" He stopped, recognising the broad Irish accent of one of the other tenants.

"Aye"

"Tell your mother I've got a remnant o' worsted for her, will ye?"

"Aye, I will. Thank ye Mrs Gallagher."

A deep male voice murmured unintelligibly from the dark.

"Stop complainin!" she snapped, "You're only payin' for what you're usin'. Get on wi' it will ye? I got a dinner to cook."

The stairs ran through three floors. The last flight of creaking timber treads led darkly to a small landing, above which was a sloping grey ceiling with a small skylight, patinated to a dull ochre by decades of filth and weather.

There were only two doors off this landing. John opened one and entered the 'L' shaped room, giving his muddied jacket a brush with his hand as he did so.

The attic room was lit by one skylight. Like the one in the hallway, it cast a dim, gingerish light into the room, its illumination supplemented by an oil lamp that sat on the table.

He could hear the splash and scrape made by his mother as she prepared vegetables out of sight, around the corner. A small poorly dressed girl of about four years ran up to greet him. "Johnnie, Johnnie! Maw! Johnnie's back." The girl recoiled when she saw him. "Ye'se filthy dirty!"

"Shh..." whispered John, with as much emphasis as is possible when trying to be quiet. "Lizzie, shut up!" He whispered, making what he hoped would be an effectively threatening grimace.

Lizzie smiled wickedly. "Maw, Johnnie's all wet and filthy dirty and stinks of pigs!"

John winced, anticipating what was to follow. His mother peered round the corner. "Johnnie! Come here..." There was a degree of menace in her tone.

"Oh Maw, Mrs Gallagher…" his clumsy attempt at changing the subject was swiftly dismissed.

"Bugger Mrs Gallagher! Look at the state o' ye!"

"He's a dirty sod, isn't he?" said Lizzie.

"And ye can shut up, Ye's nae better!" their mother chided. She took John's arm roughly and spun him around.

"For the love of God, have ye been rollin' in the sty? Get your clothes off." The 'get' was emphasised by a cuff round the head. John pulled away and protected his head with his arms.

"It was Rosie's fault, not mine," he said, in a defiantly hurt voice.

Flora, his mother, wiped her dirtied hands on her apron and continued cutting up the potatoes.

"You're no bairn now, John Paul, you're twelve years old. In a year's time ye'll be workin'. Ye should be actin' like a grown lad."

John undressed sullenly to his underwear. The uncomfortable silence was only broken by the hiss as a pot boiled over on the range, sending puffs of white steam towards the slope of the ceiling. She moved the pot to one side.

"What about Mrs Gallagher?" she asked, her voice restored to its usual calm.

John picked up on the change of tone and, believing that there was little to be gained by maintaining a 'hurt' voice, answered brightly ""Oh, she says that she has somethin' for ye."

"What?"

"I canna remember, but she says it's worse"

"Worse, what d'ye mean?"

"I've no idea."

"Oh, Johnnie Paul, ye's a useless wee laddie," she sighed. John watched her as she dropped the vegetables into the pot on the range. "Come over here by the fire, before ye catch ye's death o' cold," she said.

John sat down by the range and looked at his feet quizzically.

"How long will it be before I get some boots?"

"You're next, now Lizzie has hers," came the reply, "I canna pay more tae the boot club just now. Ye'll have them in… maybe a month or two, dependin' on your Paw's pay. I hope ye'll treat 'em better than the last pair."

"It seems a long time since I had boots."

"Aye an' at three an' six, it'll be a long time before ye get another pair, so ye'll have tae treat 'em wi' respect. I'll make sure the cobbler puts plenty o' hobnails in the soles. She sighed: "Little Annie will be needin' a pair soon. She's nearly worn out Lizzie's old ones. They won't take another repair."

She stirred the broth on the range, sat down and picked up a partly darned sock and continued weaving in the wool.

John looked at her as she rocked gently in the chair. She seemed older than her thirty-five years, or was it just the glow from the range that made her seem so?

His attention moved again to his feet. Mud had caked on his toenails and was now dry. He picked it off piece by piece and dropped it down the crack between the floorboards.

While his fingers were engaged in this activity, his mind was far away. In his stomach there was the hollow feeling of controlled excitement, as he pondered upon what tomorrow would bring.

He looked again at his mother. Would she be upset when he didn't come home after school? He didn't want to upset her. But it was all arranged now; he couldn't let the others down.

His reverie was halted abruptly by a question.

"A penny for them?" said Flora.

"Pardon?"

"A penny for your thoughts – ye seem quiet."

John tried to think of something to say and bought time to find an answer.

"Do I?" he said.

Her tone hardened. "Ye's not been fightin' at school agin' have ye?"

"No…" He searched for words. "I… I jus' feel like bein' quiet, tha's all."

"Are ye sure ye's not in trouble?"

"No, I'm fine," he said brightly.

He wondered if he ought to say anything about tomorrow, to ease his feelings of guilt, then quickly decided against it.

"Ye don't seem it."

"I'm just a wee bit tired," he lied.

"Ye spend too much time down the docks," she scolded.

"He says he wants tae be a sailor," said Lizzie, from the back of the room, where she was playing with a grubby doll.

"Aye, well, he could do worse," replied Flora. "Look how your Uncle James has got on. He's Captain of his own ship." The hint of a smile crossed her face. "Can ye see Johnnie as a sailor, Lizzie?"

"I can, if he brings me presents like Uncle James does."

"I'll bring ye back somethin' nice… and Maw an' Paw too," he said, without thinking.

"Ye make it sound like ye's sailin' tomorrow," said Flora lightly.

John coloured up and forced a chuckle, then thought that he would test the ground. "I wouldn'a mind."

Flora gently set the seal on the conversation. "Och no. School's more important right now. In a year or so maybe, if they'll have ye."

The sound of shouting could be heard from the alley below and there was a crash, as if something had been broken.

"There they go again," she said, "always someone fightin'."

A high-pitched female voice shouted incomprehensibly and the noise stopped.

"Ah well, that was a short one; takes a woman tae sort it out."

## 3.  Leaving home

The evening passed as most did. The men had returned from work for their dinners and, having eaten, went to the Inn. Later they returned and played cards for an hour or two at the table. Now everyone was asleep except for John, who was in too much of a state of nervous excitement.

The wick of the lamp had been turned down, but it gave just enough light to see around the room. A curtained off recess was where his Father and Mother slept, in a creaky iron bed. Ann was still in a cot but was getting too big now and would soon be joining the rest of the family on straw paliasses on the floor.

John listened to the breathing of the sleeping people. The low snore was his Father and other, softer snores came from lodgers, mainly sailors, who were in port. Laying on the paliasse next to John was a large, sweaty sailor whose ripe odour was tinted with the pungent perfume of strong pipe tobacco and beer. On his other side lay Lizzie, breathing softly.

The sounds of these sleepers reminded John of the sea: of waves, rising and falling endlessly. But then, everything reminded John of the sea, particularly now, when its call was so irresistable.

He looked up at the sloping ceiling. Its stains formed maps, like the one in the class at school. He made imaginary voyages nightly across the ceiling. India was there. Antigua and Jamaica too. But for the last week or so it was Canada; Quebec to be precise, that was the destination.

"Come on Johnnie, get up. I'll not tell ye again." John lifted his head and looked about him. Flora was bustling about, piling up the paliasses.

"I must have gone tae sleep." he thought.

The last thing he remembered was seeing light beginning to return through the skylight window. That must have been at about six. "What's the time Maw?" he asked huskily.

"Time ye were up and about. Up – Now!" she said firmly.

He got dressed almost in a daze, thinking of the day to come. Somehow the room looked strange, almost as if he was seeing it for the first time, or could it be the last time?

Flora clattered about irritably.

"I have tae go tae the well. Get y'sel somethin' for breakfast and do wake up and get movin'!" She took two leather buckets and left the room. John listened as the ever-quietening creak of the stairs confirmed her descent. He looked at Lizzie and Ann to check that they were still sleeping. The depth of their breathing showed that they were.

"Bread," he thought, "I'll need some bread… and cheese. I wonder, is there any meat? Some biscuits perhaps?" He rushed to the table, hacked a lump from the loaf, rummaged among the tin boxes on the shelves by the range and with loaded hands ran over and stuffed the food into the pockets of his jacket, which was hanging on a peg on the back of the door. The pockets bulged conspicuously. 'She'll notice all this,' he thought, and squeezed the pockets hard to try and compress their bulk. This had little effect.

He had never felt less like eating, but the overloaded pockets commanded that he reduce their cargo. Stuffing his hand into a pocket he pulled out a handful – a melange of bread, cheese, cold salted pork, sweet biscuit and mint humbug. Without looking he forced this into his mouth and, with difficulty, ate it. He repeated the performance, taking a handful from the other pocket.

After a while of earnest chewing, which by now was making his jaws ache, he became aware that something was resisting his teeth's best efforts. He pulled out the offending string and carried on chewing in an even more determined manner, as the creaks on the stairs announced the imminent return of Flora.

Standing at the head of the stairs to catch her breath she sighed, "Those stairs'll be the death o' me."

John was standing just inside the door, with cheeks bulging.

"In this house we sit down for meals… and do ye have tae bolt your food like that? It's revoltin'!"

Obligingly he went to the table and sat down. She brought the buckets in and placed them by the range. Having finished his mouthful John went to put his jacket on.

"You're not wearin' that jacket, laddie, not 'til it's been washed. I'm not sendin' ye tae school stinkin' like a piggery. What would people think? It's no that cold and not rainin' so ye'll survive wi'out it."

"But Maw…"

"No Johnnie. Perhaps it'll teach ye tae take more care o' your clothes in future."

The boy flicked his cap on to his head irritably and reached craftily for his jacket.

"No!" said Flora firmly. "I told ye – leave it. Don't forget your books and slate." John hesitated. "Go on boy, ye'll be late. Lord, what's the matter wi' ye lately?"

John snatched up his books and slate and cast a final glance at Flora, who stood with her arms folded, shaking her head in mock exasperation. John still felt pangs of guilt for what he was about to do, but this was sublimated, as he descended the stairs, by excitement and anticipation.

Once outside he was aware of a cold breeze. He looked over to the pig as he walked down the close. She looked up, her wet, pink snout glistening, and grunted a greeting.

"Bye Rosie" he said with a joviality that he did not feel, because he knew that by the time that he returned she would be pork and bacon, the festivity of 'Pig Day' being not far off.

John had arranged to meet his friends outside the Custom House and, with a last glance back down Buchanan's Close, he strode off towards the docks.

The breeze had lifted the curtain of fog, but the sky over Greenock was stained brown by the discharge from the poisonous chimneys that littered the skyline. As he turned into William Street he could see West Harbour and beyond it the Firth. The harbour was jammed solid, a jungle of masts and spars. Ships sat idly at anchor in three tiers outside West Harbour, and five abreast outside the East Harbour, all waiting their turn to dock.

He walked along East Breast to the corner of the Custom House. As he stood there waiting for his friends, he began to feel the bite of the strengthening breeze and the steely chill of the cobbles through the soles of his feet.

He began to shiver and wondered if this was partly due to his state of pent up excitement. 'Where is everyone?' he thought, looking around in all directions, as his teeth performed involuntary drum rolls.

It was several minutes later that he saw the familiar shapes of two of his friends walking along the quayside past the New Graving Dock into Custom House Place. He waved and they returned his greeting.

"Hello Pauley," said a tall, gangly fourteen-year-old with curly carrot-coloured hair and scruffy, threadbare clothes.

"Hello Jamie, where have ye been?" replied John, clasping his books to his chest for warmth. "Have ye seen Hughie?"

"Who, McEwan?" asked Jamie.

"Aye"

"Not since yesterday. We canna wait too long"

'Perhaps he's changed his mind and gone back tae Glasgow,' thought John.

"We have tae go soon," added Jamie, "while the crew are away from the ship. They finished loadin' last night."

"There's no been a sign o' anyone on board for a couple o' hours," said Robbie, the second boy, a thin, ragged youth who was, like John, barefooted.

"It's bloody cold, I say we ought tae get on board before we freeze tae death," said Jamie.

"Can we wait a wee bit longer," pleaded John, "I'm sure Hughie will come; just five minutes…"

Five minutes later they were still waiting, shuffling from foot to foot, with shoulders hunched and hands pressed deep into their pockets.

"Look Pauley, we had a plan, he's no comin,'" said Jamie firmly, "I'm gonna see if the coast is clear an' if it is, I'm goin on board. If ye wanna come, come now or ye can sort y'sel out."

"I'm wi ye…" said Robbie, and they loped off towards Victoria Harbour.

John scanned the docks, desperate for a sign of his friend. He was looking intently among the clutter and activity of East Breast when he heard a familiar voice behind him.

"Johnnie…" shouted Hughie, breathlessly. He was bent over with his hands resting on his knees.

"Where have ye been? I've been here hours," John exaggerated.

"This errand … took longer … than I thought … couldn't get here any sooner … I…"

"Come on then," interrupted John, "if we hurry we can catch Jamie and Robbie before they get on board."

He ran off down the quayside. Hughie wearily followed on, desperately trying to keep up.

## 4.  At the dockside

They arrived at Victoria Harbour to find their two friends standing behind a head high stack of timber. Jamie was peering over the top as the latecomers joined them.

"He's comin' down now," said Jamie as he turned.

"Oh ye did decide tae come after all, did ye?"

"It wasna my fault... I had tae run an errand," gasped Hughie, in a high, thin voice.

"Wha's happenin'?" asked John.

"There was a sailor aloft, fiddlin' wi' one o' the brace blocks. He's comin down now. We'll have tae bide awhile."

Now that the time to board the Arran was getting close John began to wonder whether or not he should go. He looked at the ship: although not a large vessel she was nevertheless impressive. The black paint of her sides only thinly masked the scars of twelve years at sea. Built for utilitarian purposes, she was undecorated on her stern, with only the words Arran, and underneath in smaller letters, Greenock. A rubbing bar ran the length of the ship at gunwale level. This relieved the austerity of the hull and, where paint remained, it was white.

The masts seemed much taller than John remembered them. They were painted white up to 'top' level, with topmasts and topgallant masts of orange-coloured, varnished Vancouver pine. The ship was square rigged, with heavy black painted yards, on which grey sails were neatly furled.

From the masts and spars came a cobweb of rigging. John wondered how anyone could know what rope did what. Would they expect him to climb the rigging? He hoped not. What would the Captain do when they were found? Would he beat them – or put them in irons – or throw them overboard – surely not?

The gusting wind caused the ropes and wires to whine and moan, a sound which did little to relieve his feelings of disquiet.

The Arran looked very serious and not a little intimidating, perhaps, all in all, not the vessel for a pleasure sail. Jamie had told John earlier that her master was a kindly man, but he could not dispel the feeling of foreboding and sought to find an excuse to stay behind.

He thought, 'Perhaps I should wait 'til I'm thirteen. I can go to sea wi' Maw's blessin' then.' He looked at Hughie, who was peering round the edge of the stack of timber.

"Hughie?" said John quietly; the boy turned around. "D'ye think we should go?"

Hughie shrugged his shoulders carelessly. "I'll go if ye will."

John wondered how his friend would cope with the rigours of sea life. He was painfully thin with pale skin and light brown hair. At the age of eight he had been touched by the cholera epidemic that had ravaged Greenock, and was often away from school. Everyone agreed that he was lucky to have survived.

"He's gone ashore," said Jamie, excitedly, from his look out, "We'll give him a minute, then get on board"

Neither John or Hughie moved. They searched each other's faces for support. Finally, Hughie spoke, the expression in his blue eyes confirming his words. "We'll be alright. Jamie's wi' us. He knows what he's doin'"

"Come on you two," called Jamie urgently, "let's go see the world!"

These bold words, promising comradeship and adventure, dispelled John's fears. "Aye, let's go see the world," he smiled. The decision was made.

"Your books. What about your books?" asked Hughie.

John peered over the edge of the quay and looked impishly at his friend. One by one, he dropped the books, and finally his slate into the water and, for a second, watched them bobbing among the sludge and debris that lapped at the stone harbour wall.

Now his bridges were burnt.

The sight of boys boarding a ship was not unusual. The docks were a magnet to children who would help unload the ships, run errands and do little jobs in exchange for money, food or other gifts. During school holidays the docks were virtually overrun with them.

With the bustle on the dockside, of wagons coming and going, the shouting of dockers and the sound of hooves on cobbles, no-one noticed the four boys, one by one ascend the gangway to the Arran.

"We must split up," whispered Jamie, as they crouched by the coamings of the main hold.

"Robbie an' me'll go into the main hold here, you two better find somewhere else tae go." John felt more than a little betrayed and frightened about being excluded.

"Why can't we all stay together?" he asked.

"Because we'll be found if we do; we have tae spread ourselves thin. That way we all get a chance o' gettin' away wi it. Now do as you're told an' go hide somewhere else… Now."

John hesitated. There was a hint of hostility in Jamie's voice that he had not heard before. Suddenly he felt very vulnerable, despite Hughie's company.

"Go on, bugger off," said Jamie irritably, waving them away.

"C'mon Hughie, let's go an find somewhere tae hide," John grumbled. "I bet we find a better place than their rotten old hold." Hughie followed on silently. They crept rather aimlessly for'ard until they reached the forecastle head.

"Shall we go under here?" whispered John, who then peered into the gloom of the three-foot-high under-deck area.

"What's under there?" whispered Hughie in return.

"Tons o' stuff." They edged carefully past the windlass and, crouching, went into the dark area under the raised deck.

Once inside, they stopped to allow their eyes to adjust to the gloom.

"Stinks a bit," breathed Hughie.

"Shh…" Hughie was clasping his friend's shirt sleeve tightly and John could feel that he was trembling.

John put his mouth to his friend's ear. "See that pile o' rope?" He pointed. "Let's see if we can hide there."

They stepped over the anchor chain and edged past the paint locker. They found that what appeared to be a pile of rope was, in fact, a pile of timber blocks over which some canvas and rope had been thrown.

They pulled the wood blocks towards them and built a barricade, on top of which they dragged some of the canvas and rope. From outside, their hiding place looked exactly like a pile of odds and ends, but there did not seem enough space to hide one boy, let alone two.

Soon the lads began to get hot in the confined space. John moved one or two of the timbers, primarily for air, but also so that he could see, through a small gap, past the windlass to the deck, although his view was restricted by the side of the paint store, the deck house and the low ceiling of the deck above.

After a while of sitting and talking in whispers, they heard men's voices and the sound of feet on the deck. Both the boys jumped in fear as a sailor's legs suddenly appeared by the windlass.

In the close confines of the hiding place they could hear each other's hearts beating and were certain that the sailor must be able to hear them too. The man climbed up on to the forecastle head and, a minute later, again made the boy's hearts miss a beat, when he jumped down on to the main deck and threw a small pulley into the dark of their hiding place. This struck the boys' barricade. When he had gone they panted in relief and continued to listen as the crew moved about the ship. Before long, the hiding place became very stuffy and the boys were sweating. They moved some of the canvas, which allowed air to circulate better.

During the next few hours the forecastle area was momentarily visited several times by the crew. The boys began to welcome these visits as a break from the monotony of waiting.

A stifled sneeze broke the silence in the gloom.

"Shh…" whispered John.

"It wasna me," whispered Hughie. Even in the dim light John could see from Hughie's expression that he, too, realised that they were not alone.

The ship's hands came and went and muffled snatches of conversation could be heard. A sailor approached the forecastle head carrying a lamp. He had no sooner arrived than another seaman's blue trousered legs were framed in the opening.

"That's three of the buggers so far," said the legs, Have a good look or there'll be trouble. Ye ken what Kerr's like."

The blue-trousered sailor then walked off towards the stern and beyond him John noticed activity by the gangway. His view was limited by the deckhouse, but a large sailor was with two other people. He thought he saw a flash of ginger hair. However, the boy's attention was concentrated more on the seaman by the forecastle. The large man bent down, held the lamp in front of him and peered past the paint store in a menacing way. His features seemed to move and become distorted by the swaying light of the lamp. He then edged under the low deck and crawled past their hiding place and out of John's vision. Only the sound of him moving among the storage told of where he was. Gradually he came closer and both boys flinched as something struck their barricade. After this, the boys saw him crawl once more into the light and stroll off towards the stern.

The activity increased during the following hours. The boys, in their dark hideaway, could see some of what was happening outside. Grating noises could be felt, as much as heard, through the ship's timbers and Hughie felt something small but solid drop on to the side of his nose. He probably would not have thought twice about it, except that whatever it was, with tiny feet, ran across his cheek and down his neck. He quickly brushed it off.

The crew seemed totally occupied with their work in preparing the ship for sea and the boys, for the first time, felt relaxed and optimistic about the coming voyage despite the consciousness that someone else, or perhaps others, were hidden no more than a few feet away.

Any conversation was in whispers and the only movement they permitted themselves was to change their postures slightly to relieve 'pins and needles'.

It was now four hours since they went into hiding. John felt Hughie move a little, then he again became still, but there was a new sound in the dark; the sound of crunching.

"Are y'eatin' somethin'?" he whispered.

"Mmm" was the response.

"What is it?"

"A biscuit."

"Gi' us a bit then."

"I havena' got much," breathed Hughie, biting off another piece.

"Oh, gi' us a bit," pleaded John, "I've nothin at all."

Hughie sighed, and a piece of biscuit was clumsily passed over in the gloom.

"Thanks, I'm starvin'" he said, gnawing at the hard biscuit as quietly as he could.

"Why didn't ye bring somethin' tae eat?" asked Hughie.

"Couldn't get it out o' the house," he replied. In his mind he could see his jacket, the pockets bulging, hanging on the door at home.

Someone walked on the deck over their heads and for several minutes clattered about. The boys could hear the sound of voices, but could not make out what was being said.

An intermittent creaking sound began and they were aware of movement for the first time. A small anxious thrill went through John as he realised that the familiar 'knock-knock' sound was the steam tug. As the sound did not recede he guessed that it was their ship that was being towed. They were on their way.

## 5. The voyage begins

The pitching and rolling of the ship deepened as time went on and the boys could hear the waves grumbling against the bows. In their gloomy hideaway they could see little, but were acutely aware of the vessel's insistent dance. Their initial good humour and excitement gradually gave way to other sensations.

"Oh God, I feel sick," murmured Hughie.

"Ye's not goin' tae be sick are ye?" responded John who shared the same incipient feelings.

"I don't know, I feel rotten."

"I feel rotten too, an' I'm dyin' for a pee…"

A sudden shouting drew their attention.

"For God's sake check again! That's two more o' the brats found. Use your eyes, damn you! Hunter, check the fo'c's'le"

A terse voice answered, "We've bin' down there playin' cards. There's no-one in there."

"Then check under the fo'c's'le head again."

"Aye Mister Kerr," said the sailor. He crouched down and peered into the dark area where the boys were hidden.

"Can't see a bloody thing!" the sailor muttered to himself, "Oh tae hell wi' it. There's no-one there."

A few minutes later the ship began to pitch and roll slackly, like a log, and the sound of the tug grew closer. Through their peephole, the lads could see the smoke from her funnel drifting across the Arran's deck and could smell its sulphur breath.

The day was beginning to fade and a chorus of unintelligible orders, echoed by the recipients, sang out against the sigh of the wind in the rigging. The activity on deck was intense. John saw crew members running hither and thither, climbing the shrouds and hauling on lines of rope, clinging like spiders to a web.

The dry flapping of canvas and the sonorous creaking of the timbers, as the masts and yards took the strain of the wind in the rippling sails, gave the ship an entirely new feel.

Yards were lifted into position, topsails set and the helm was brought round to gain best effect from the wind. Sails filled with a shudder and crack of canvas and the ship heeled sharply over to port. This alarmed Hughie.

"Oh Lord, we're sinkin!" he said out loud.

"Shh!" scolded John, equally worried by the lurch of the Arran. They clung to each other with clammy hands.

The steam whistle of the tug sounded in the distance and the sound of its engine faded away.

Once the boys had become used to the angle of the ship they felt that, at least, the rolling had lessened, but the pitching, if anything was more severe and the ship seemed more 'bows down' in the water than previously.

From their hiding place, they could see a tiny patch of sky. This was now deepening in tone and its clouds had a distinctly orange tinge.

"Can we go out o' here now?" said Hughie

"It'll be dark soon."

"We'll make a move in a while. The tug's gone but we better bide a bit, or they might call it back... I'm burstin' for a pee."

"So am I, an' I feel awful sick."

"I don't feel so good either," replied John.

There was now a sudden urgency in Hughie's voice. "I gotta get out o' here now, let me out. Oh Johnnie, I'm goin tae be sick!"

"Oh Christ!" exclaimed John, pushing the barricade aside and scrambling over its debris.

"Are ye alright Hughie?" he asked from a safe distance. The sound of retching answered his question. John fought against the urge to be sick in sympathy.

Suddenly John's arm was grasped by a strong hand and he was dragged out into the light of the open deck.

"And who the hell are you?" said the sailor, who he recognised as the man who had searched their hiding place earlier. The boy was about to answer when further muffled sounds of vomiting came from the dark under the deck.

"Whoever's under there come out now or I'll come in and get ye."

Hughie struggled past the windlass on to the open deck, wiping his mouth on his sleeve as he did so. He was visibly trembling and stood, head down and crying.

The sailor's tone softened. "Alright lad, I'll no harm ye." A movement behind Hughie drew his attention.

"Christ Almighty, how many more of ye?"

A boy, as small as the other two, but a little more thickset, picked his way cautiously onto the deck and squinted in the light. John, amazed, was quick to disclaim him.

"He's nothin' tae do wi' us. We didna' know he was there."

Jimmy McGinnes, like John was barefoot and his clothes were in a very poor state. His trousers and jacket were a network of holes through which his skin could be seen. The fair hair which protruded like trodden straw from his cap, was matted and his face was weathered, with dull crimson cheeks and small eyes. He carried a small satchel.

'How many more o' ye?" asked the sailor angrily, pushing past the boys to peer into the dark. "Come out now, or I'll gi' ye a rope's end!" he shouted into the void. There was no response. "Ye can thank your stars it was me, not the Mate, who found ye," he said to the boys. "Ye stay here, mind, an' I'll go an see if Mister Niven wants ye put wi' the other two."

'Other two,' thought John to himself. 'That'll be Jamie and Robbie, I bet.' He discounted the red hair he had seen at the gangway before the ship sailed. The boys were now obviously in dire need of relieving themselves.

"For God's sake use the bog house," said the sailor, pointing at a tall narrow cubicle by the side of the ship, "before ye wet y'sels."

"Aye Sir," said John, diving into the cubicle, closely followed by the other two.

When the sailor returned all three were standing, shivering, on the open deck.

"Ye's tae come wi' me tae the fo'c's'le tonight. Are ye hungry?"

The events of the last few minutes had effectively dispelled the feeling of sea sickness and all three, though still feeling queasy were, all the same, quite hungry.

"If ye've a wee something," piped John, "I'd be glad o' it, Sir."

"Follow me," said the sailor. The boys, staggering against the ship's motion, tottered after him.

He opened the galley door and went inside, reappearing with a handful of buff-coloured, round biscuits, about three inches in diameter and three quarters of an inch thick.

"Here y'are lads, one each. Now let's get ye tae bed. John looked quizzically at the biscuit and nibbled at the edge.

"It's a wee bit hard…" he mumbled, "and what's this black thing?" He touched it and it moved quickly to the edge of the biscuit and fell off.

"Hughie," he said, "a black crawly thing's just come out o' my biscuit."

"Where?" said Hughie, peering closely at it.

"Where is it?" asked Jimmy.

"It's on the deck somewhere."

They all scanned the deck for signs of it.

"What've ye lost?" asked the seaman.

"Somethin's just dropped off ma biscuit," said John.

"Black was it?"

"Aye."

"I didna tell ye, did I? They're little weevils, they're in all the biscuits. Knock 'em out on the deck." He took John's biscuit and tapped it on the scrubbed deck. Several small black insects fell out.

"There, see?" said the sailor.

"Ugh!" said Hughie, grimacing and sticking out his tongue with distaste. John examined his biscuit closely while the others tapped theirs on the deck.

"How many have ye got?" asked John.

"Tons," said Hughie, stamping on the offending creatures and examining the remains.

"Seven," said Jimmy, more realistically. The sailor led the youngsters back toward the bows and to the companionway that led down to the crew's accommodation in the forecastle.

The boys, in turn, carefully descended the steep and tilted ladder into a stifling and dense fug of sickly tobacco smoke. A lamp cast a yellow light on to a small table, around which sat several sailors.

"They're too small," said one, acknowledging their arrival, "Throw 'em back!" The others laughed.

"Three more. That's five o' the buggers," said another. John and Hughie looked at each other.

"The other two are bound tae be Jamie an' Robbie" said John.

"I don't think so – look over there." Hughie pointed to a round-faced, poorly dressed man and a reasonably clad, reddish-haired boy of much their own age. They had seen neither of them before. Both were sitting motionless and limp, against a bunk by the apex of the triangular room. They looked unwell and hung their heads, concerned only with their own misery. They barely noticed the arrival of the three boys.

"Is that the other two?" asked John of the sailor.

"Aye," he replied, "Oh, look at the colour of them, I'll get some buckets.

He climbed the companionway and upon collecting three buckets from the sail room, met the carpenter, who had two more youths with him.

"Hey Rob, where d'ye find those?"

"I was battenin' down the forehatch and out they came."

"Tha's seven now. We're rainin' stowaways!"

"Aye, I know."

"An' four o' them hardly more than bairns."

"Wait 'til Mister Kerr finds out. Ye'll hear him in Aberdeen!"

"Oh, bugger me, not more guttersnipes?" exclaimed a sailor in disbelief as they, too, descended into the forecastle.

"Can't ye find us a few buxom girlies?" said another. "Hey! You're out o' turn, it's my hand."

John was not too disappointed to see others, as it seemed to him that there was a certain safety in numbers. They too, joined the other stowaways with a silent, almost disinterested, nod of acknowledgement.

John looked at them. What a motley bunch they seemed; hardly his idea of fellow fortune seekers. The man, Barney Reilly, was thin and wore a battered low crowned bowler hat. He was unshaven and in grubby, threadbare clothes. The few words that he had spoken declared him to be Irish. Then there were the two newcomers. John guessed that they were about sixteen or so. Davie Brand was quite well clothed and fairly clean looking, with a serious way about him. James Bryson was taller, at about six feet and the more thickset of the two. His face, scarred by smallpox, was unshaven and dirty. He smelled sweetly sweaty and his clothes were more grubby than threadbare. There was an air of insolent arrogance about him.

Peter Currie had been with Reilly when John, Hughie and Jimmy entered the forecastle. He had red/gold coloured hair and a mass of freckles on his face. He was a quiet boy, clothed reasonably well, and a little taller than John, Hughie and Jimmy.

"What d'ye reckon Mister Kerr will do wi' em?" asked a sailor with bad teeth, just loudly enough, so that the stowaways would hear. John took the bait and listened intently to the conversation.

"The same as he's done before wi' other stowboys, I suppose," said another, dealing a hand of cards with a dismissive air.

"You don't mean...?" said the bad teeth. He stopped and circled his hand in the air as if searching for the right word.

"I do."

"What, even the wee ones?"

"Especially the wee ones." He looked over to the smaller boys who were listening, wide eyed with trepidation, at the repartee.

"They say the sharks prefer the young'uns. More tender, I think they say. Their bones is more crunchy too, than big'uns."

"Is that so?"

"Aye, I believe it is."

"Take no notice o'em boys," said another sailor laying on his bunk, "They're havin' fun wi' ye."

"Wouldn't dream o' it!" grinned Bad Teeth.

The companionway doors opened wide and some of the fug funnelled out in the gasp of wind. The Steward, in sunset stained white jacket stood in the doorway with a tray of steaming metal pans. This was handed down to a sailor. The table was cleared quickly and stools dragged around it.

"Eat well men," he said, "Looks like ye's got a cold and rough watch ahead o' ye."

A sailor moved from his bunk to the table.

"Don't worry lads, I'll make sure we leave some for ye." The men began eating their food with obvious relish. The boys, all of whom still felt sick, could hardly bear the smell of the food, let alone watch the seamen eating it.

"Come on lads, said the sailor, help y'sels. There's plenty here. Ye've hard work ahead. Ye have tae eat."

None of the stowaways moved.

"Just try a little," he continued, "It'll make ye feel better. Ye feel ill cause ye's hungry. Come and have some biscuit an' butter."

John, Jimmy and Brand went quietly over to the table and were given some biscuit, butter, beef and potatoes. None of them could manage more than a mouthful or two. Bad Teeth and his friend made a point of eating in the noisiest way possible, to the amusement of the other seamen. They were slobbering and slurping and watching the effect on the faces of the suffering youngsters, who tried without success to shut their minds to it.

"Any more o' that delicious pig fat, Jeremiah?"

"Aye, d'ye want me tae roll it in the butter for ye?" came the reply.

Brand caught the eye of the kind sailor. "Where do we sleep?" he asked, as much to break the banter as for any other reason.

"Mister Niven – he's the second mate – says you're tae sleep on the floor under the bunks; there's some mats in the corner tae lie on."

"Could have asked us first," grumbled a card player.

"Does he ever?" said another.

"If I get lice off 'em there'll be trouble," said yet another.

Even before the meal was over, Jimmy vomited into a bucket and before long all the stowaways were being sick.

"Bloody good job we're on watch soon. I would nae fancy this all night," said a sailor, struggling into his oilskins.

"I don't know why we have tae put up wi'em at all," said another.

The watch changed and the off-duty crew entered the forecastle. They ate and played cards for a while, largely ignoring their unwelcome room mates, but grumbling and complaining when they vomited. For the stowaways the night was long, broken by bouts of seasickness. The sharp sound of violent retching punctuated the calm of rounded, gentle snores, breaking the sleep of the off duty watch.

As the first weak beams of daylight entered the tiny portholes of the forecastle, John saw Brand struggle out from beneath a bunk, ascend the companionway to the deck and close the door quietly behind him. For a while John watched the beams of light scan up and down the wall of the cabin. He felt battered. His throat was burning, his chest felt bruised and he felt clammy all over. Despite being sick more times than he could remember, there seemed to be no relief from this feeling of nausea.

'Perhaps some fresh air may help me feel better' he thought. Pulling himself out from under the bunk he then stood up, and was surprised at how weak he felt. Wearily, he climbed the steps to the deck and upon opening the companionway door saw sailors in oilskins walking toward the stern of the ship. It was raining and the strong chill wind bit and tore at his thin shirt. Davie Brand was leant on the Arran's rail, looking out to sea.

This was the first proper view that John had seen of the ship under sail. The decks were wet and over the port side he could see the pitted, leaden ocean dashing against the Arran's bulwarks, casting fans of white water into the air, to be swept away by the wind.

The sails, a glossy dark grey, surged stiffly with effort and the rigging shivered and moaned in sympathy.

Sharp needles of rain drove him back down into the warmth of the forecastle. He realised that he was both ill-prepared and ill-clothed for such a life, and wondered why on earth he had wanted to come on such a voyage. Feeling quite sorry for himself, he crawled back on to his mat under a bunk and quietly cried himself to sleep.

# 6. *The stowaways meet the Captain and Mate*

A sudden dig in the ribs from a none-too-gentle boot roused John from his sleep. He looked blearily up at the seaman.

"Up – now. Mr Kerr wants to see ye." The other stowaways, ashen and stiff from sleep, were struggling to their feet from under the bunks. This was made more difficult by the roll of the ship.

"Good God, what will he make of ye?" he continued, "Hangin' on tae the bunks like a bunch o' women. Come wi' me."

The stowaways, fighting to keep their balance climbed the companionway to the open deck. It was spitting with rain, driven by a biting wind from the stern of the ship.

The boys were ushered along the length of the deck towards the poop. Their progress was in the form of short, staggering, zig-zag bursts, as they attempted to counter the gyrations of the deck. Spray salted their lips and jewelled their hair. John sorely missed the protection of his jacket.

"Wait here," ordered the seaman, who disappeared into the stern quarters. John looked at Hughie, who had a brownish smear around his mouth.

"What ye bin eatin'?" he asked in a hoarse voice. Hughie's voice was broken and hardly audible above the noise of ship and sea.

"Nothin' "

"What's that brown stuff round your mouth then?"

"Dunno," said Hughie, trying to wipe it off and looking at his hand.

The sailor emerged from the stern companionway and brushed past the boys as if they weren't there. Behind him, a figure appeared in the doorway to the stern quarters. He was dressed in a brass buttoned reefer jacket. In his early thirties, he was perhaps five feet seven, with black hair, a dark full beard and coarse features. Although a thin man, he had the complexion and puffiness of face of a hardened drinker. He looked tough.

"Follow me," he ordered gruffly. The stowaways descended the short ladder into a small panelled timber lobby with five doors. The officer knocked on the one opposite the companionway.

"Come in," came the response. The officer stood aside and waved the stowaways into the saloon, followed them in and closed the door.

The Captain sat at the desk with charts spread on the table in front of him; a slim man of about twenty-eight, he stood up, his chair grating against the floor. His features were finely chiselled and his brown hair, moustache and beard were immaculately groomed. He looked at the stowaways in turn. They all avoided looking back at him.

"Why are ye here?" he demanded in a firm voice. No one answered.

"You," he said, pointing at John. He beckoned. John stepped forward, whereupon the Captain grabbed him by the shirt front and shook him, causing the boy to lose his balance.

"What are ye doing here?"

"Please Sir, we want to be sailors."

"Ha!" spat the Captain with contempt, pushing John away.

"Have ye eaten since ye've been on board?" The lads mumbled that they hadn't had much to eat.

"Well ye need no expect much from me. Ye all are here wi'out permission. I'll not gi'ye a free ride. Ye'll work, and work hard to earn your grub. If ye work hard yell be treated fair. If ye don't, ye can expect trouble. Mister Kerr here is my First Mate, he'll make sure ye get the treatment ye deserve. Ye'll call everyone on this ship 'sir', includin' the seamen and ye'll do as ye's told."

He sat down, picked up a pair of dividers and toyed with them.

"Ye'll not enter these quarters ever, except by invitation by Mister Kerr or mysel' and ye must not go into the foc's'le except tae sleep. Y'understand?" The boys nodded and grunted a response.

"Mister Kerr, take them to the cook for somethin' tae eat."

"Aye Captain," said Kerr, brusquely, waving the boys out of the cabin.

Since their discovery the boys had eaten very little and would normally have been ravenous, but the motion of the ship was still having its nauseous effect. The boys had only just gained the deck when Jimmy McGinnes was sick. His vomiting affected Currie and Hughie, who also began to retch, but by this time very little more than bile was being brought up and this seared the boys' already sore throats. Hughie retched a second time and his sputum-like vomit was strongly streaked with blood. The other boys clearly looked unwell.

"Ye no want somethin tae eat?" asked Kerr.

The boys all mumbled that they didn't.

"Then ye can get up an appetite wi' a bit o' work." He slapped his hand hard on Hughie's shoulder. The boy's knees gave way under the blow.

"Ye can start by washing this lot away. Ye'll find a bucket and brooms in the sail locker. Ye can fill the bucket from the pump on the side o' the water closet."

Hughie wiped his mouth, his hand shaking with exertion.

Kerr dispersed the boys to work in different parts of the ship. Brand was first given the job of scraping spars, then later, being the cleanest looking, was sent to help the cook. Currie, Jimmy and John were given the task of scraping the decking of the forecastle head while Bryson and Reilly manned the bilge pumps.

Hughie tottered aft with bucket in one hand and broom in the other. A minor shift of course caused an unexpected change in the ship's rhythm. Hughie lost his balance, fell over the bucket and rolled into the gulley that travelled the length of the ship by the rail. This was running with seawater and he became soaked to the skin down one side of his body. He fell heavily against the ship's side. To his surprise, an opening appeared and he half fell through it. He was grabbed by a seaman, who pulled him gasping to his feet.

"Tha's a stupid place tae put a hatch," panted the boy, "I could o' fallen in the sea." He looked back at the steel top hinged flap which opened and closed a little with the roll of the ship. "What's it there for anyway?"

"Tha's a freein' port," the sailor motioned. "They're all along the sides o' the ship. When the deck's swamped by the sea they let it out again."

"Nearly let me out too!" said Hughie.

"Aye, well, The Arran wasnae built for wee boys like y'sel'. First rule o' the sea laddie, one hand for the ship an' one for y'sel."

For some reason that he couldn't understand, Jimmy was drawn to Bryson. It may have been that the youth's temperament was similar to his father's, or perhaps he thought that Bryson would make the best protector. He also felt sorry for him. No-one else seemed to like him. Davie Brand and Barney Reilly had quickly paired up and were too old anyway; John and Hughie were already pals and when Jimmy McGinnes had tried to befriend John, Hughie had made it clear that there wasn't room for a three way friendship. He didn't take to Peter Currie; he hardly spoke unless spoken to and seemed to want to spend his off duty time with the crew.

So he was a little disappointed when told that he was to work with John and Hughie, scraping spars by the aft deck house. Here they could be watched by any of the officers, whose habit it was to stand on the poop deck.

It seemed like hours before the darkening of the low, grey sky indicated the approach of night. A seaman came to the poop rail and shouted to the boys. "Mister Kerr says ye can stand down now for your grub." The boys dropped down to the deck and walked to the galley. The other stowaways were already there. All but Brand were exhausted, soaked and white with cold.

Plates of steaming stew were handed out to the boys. None had much appetite and the smell of the food, which normally would have made their mouths water, was sickly and unappealing. But they had to eat. John, Brand, Jimmy and Bryson sat on the hatch cover and ate the rich, brown beef stew without enthusiasm. The hard biscuits were first knocked on the deck, then softened by dipping them in the hot gravy.

Reilly, Currie and Hughie, none of whom could face eating, sheltered from the buffeting wind in the lee of the deckhouse. A figure in greatcoat and cap approached from the stern of the ship.

"Watch out, Kerr's coming," warned Bryson slyly. The mate stopped briefly by the boys.

"Ye'll not sleep in the foc's'le now," he said coldly, "the men don't want ye there. Ye can go tae the sail room. Go there when ye've eaten. I want ye on watch at four tomorrow, so get your heads down." He went to continue his walk forward.

"Sir, our clothes is soaked," said Reilly.

"Is there any place we can get them dry?"

"Ye've nae spare clothes?" This was said more as a statement than a question.

"I've surely not Sir, is there any we could borrow?"

"I could do with a coat," interjected John.

"This is a merchant ship, not a gent's outfitters. Ye'll have to wear them dry an' ye'll have tae go cold if ye've nae others."

"Miserable bastard," murmured Bryson as Kerr walked off. The wind must have carried his voice, for Kerr stopped, turned and walked slowly back to the group.

"Someone got somethin' tae say?" His voice was quietly menacing.

Bryson replied irritably, "Well, ye could try tae help us."

"Sir – Ye'll address me as Sir."

"Sir," responded Bryson, with more than a hint of contempt in his voice. Kerr kicked the dish of stew from Bryson's hands, sending it clattering across the hatch cover. The stew went in all directions. Bryson jumped up angrily, wiping splashes from his face, but was checked by Brand. Kerr went right up to Bryson, who was a good five inches taller. The lad could smell the whisky on his breath.

"I don't need a Greenock brat like you tae tell me my business. Clean that mess up now." Bryson watched scornfully as Kerr walked away. When he was clearly out of earshot he spoke.

"I'm goin tae have that little bastard."

"Oh yeah?" said Brand.

"He's nothin'. It'd be easy. I'll do it now"

Davie Brand blocked his way. "Don't be so bloody stupid. You make trouble an' we'll all suffer for it. Just calm down, stay out of his way and keep your mouth shut."

"Don't you tell me what tae do, Brand. You're not my master and neither is he." Bryson sniffed sharply, hawked and spat in the direction of Kerr, but didn't follow him.

John and the other younger ones were a little frightened by the aggression of the past few minutes and food was forgotten.

Barney Reilly joined in the conversation. "Sure, ye'd be wise to follow Davie's advice. Did ye not see that the man was as cool as ice? If he acts like that when he's calm, I wouldn't like to be there when his dander's up." Reilly sensed that Bryson was not listening, but inwardly planning his revenge. He tried to snap him out of it, putting a friendly hand on his shoulder.

"C'mon James, I'll give youse a hand to clear this mess up."

"I'm not clearin up nothin'!" sneered Bryson, shrugging off Reilly's hand. Muttering, he sauntered away to the sailroom, his fists clenched. Jimmy trotted after him. Less than a minute later Kerr walked casually back towards the stern, his face lit by the yellow light from the galley lamp as he passed by. John felt a feathery tendril of fear crawl down his back as his eyes momentarily met the Mate's. He watched the greatcoated figure walk first past the main hatch, then beyond the main mast and under the skid beams of the rear deckhouse, which housed the sail room. He wondered if Kerr would go in to find Bryson. Perhaps he had heard what Bryson had said. Perhaps Bryson was waiting for him. But no, the figure walked steadily past the deckhouse, up the steps to the poop and down into the stern quarters. Suddenly John was aware how cold he felt, and shuddered involuntarily.

The remains of the stew, now cold and coagulating, were thrown over the side of the ship and the smaller boys, tired, wet and cold, headed for the sailroom. Brand and Reilly stayed behind to clean up. John and Hughie walked together.

"I don't like this," said Hughie, on the verge of tears.

"It's not at all like I thought it was gonna be. Why are the treatin' us like this? Why is everyone so nasty? I thought this was goin' tae be a pleasure sail, but I'm ill and cold and wet an' my hands are blistered from the scrapin'. I miss my Ma an' I want tae go home."

John didn't say anything, but put his arm round the boy's shoulder and pulled him to him. In truth, his heart was as heavy as his friend's.

Using sails and coils of rope the stowaways made themselves comfortable. Away from the wind and rain John began to feel better. In fact he felt quite cosy, snuggled in a browny grey sail with another as a pillow.

The door opened and Brand and Reilly came in.

"Don't worry y'sel Bryson, Davie Brand and I have cleared up the mess for youse." There was no acknowledgement.

Brand lay down next to Bryson. "Move your arse," he said, "I need a bit of room too."

They were all very cramped together but it was better than sleeping on a rope mat under a bunk. He and Hughie, shaking with cold, huddled together for warmth. As John was quite used to sleeping alongside lodgers of every description, it seemed almost like home. Gradually they thawed out and fell asleep.

## 7. *The hardships begin*

They had, it seemed, hardly got to sleep before they were brought into consciousness by the gruff voice of a seaman.

"Come on then, it's eight bells – four o' clock, get tae work."

There was the faintest hint of a light in the sky and from the pattering sound on the window, it was still raining. The stowaways all stirred and were grunting and groaning, as if about to get up, but no one actually did and the sail room again went quiet.

The quiet was loaded. They were playing for time, dreading the inevitability of being forced out into the rain. Minutes later the sound of feet upon the deck heralded the end of their stolen time. The door of the room flew open and a seaman, lamp in hand, ordered them to get up, prodding them with a stick and motivating them with threats. The little boys obeyed immediately but the older ones were more reluctant and roused themselves slowly. Bryson made no attempt to get up.

John sensed that trouble was coming and stood well back against the damp wall of the deckhouse.

"You! Up. Now," ordered the seaman to the curled form, almost invisible among the sails. Each word was accompanied by a firm stab with the stick. Muffled obscenities from Bryson were heard by the sailor, who then increased the force of the repeated prods.

"Come... on... you... idle... good... for... nothing... brat... Get... up... you..."

Bryson suddenly, with a stream of invective, leapt to his feet and started towards the sailor. Reilly barred his way, but the youth knocked him away with a backhanded slap to the mouth. However, before Bryson could continue his attack, the seaman delivered a powerful blow to the stomach with his stick, bringing Bryson gasping, to his knees.

"Just get up!" ordered the sailor, walking away. Bryson sullenly complied, muttering under his breath.

"Another one that you're goin' to get back?" asked Brand, cheekily.

The day went slowly for the stowaways. Again Brand was sent to help the cook and the boys were dispersed in various activities. Jimmy and Bryson were put to work in the main hold, tidying the stowage that had moved in the heavy seas.

Since Bryson had first seen Jimmy he had been curious about what he kept in his small satchel.

"What's in the wee bag?" he asked.

"Nothin' much." said Jimmy defensively.

"Gi' us a look then."

Jimmy hesitated. "It's sorta private."

"Oh, go on, ye can show me." Before the boy could protest he took hold of the satchel, opened it, peered inside and tipped the contents out on to the top of a keg. There was a piece of folded paper, a letter and a small cloth bag with a drawstring. Bryson's attention immediately turned to this bag. He opened it and tipped out its contents: a dented penny and a white metal ring. Jimmy became concerned when Bryson picked up the ring and tried it on his finger.

"Can I have it back please?" he said timidly.

"Just a minute, I'm lookin' at it," Bryson said, removing it from his finger and peering closely at it.

"Is it silver?"

"I don't know. It was my pa's – he died, an' it's the only precious thing I have of his." He again stretched out his hand for the ring.

Bryson moved away a little. "Looks like silver. These are strange decorations on it. I wonder where it's from. It could be valuable – I'd better look after it for ye."

There was a hint of panic in Jimmy's voice. "No, it's alright, I can look after it."

Bryson flicked it carelessly back on to the keg. "Don't blame me if it gets stolen. I would have looked after it for ye." He unfolded the paper. On it was a drawing of a man's head and shoulders.

"That's my pa – my ma's good at drawin'. She made him sit while she did it."

Bryson barely looked at it and put it aside. He picked up the letter, opened it briefly to see if anything had been folded within it, then dropped it.

"My pa wrote tae me from sea."

Bryson's attention turned to the penny, which was badly dished.

"Wha's the penny for, how's it got like this?"

"Pa said it stopped a musket ball when he was in the Crimea. It saved his life. It was his lucky penny – now it's mine."

"Ye say your pa's dead?"

"Aye, died of cholera three years ago."

"Can't have been that lucky then, can it?" Bryson smirked, thrusting the penny into Jimmy's outstretched hand.

"Are ye sure ye don't want me tae look after the ring for ye? I don't mind."

"No, its alright, I keep it wi me all the time and it's safe in its wee bag."

Jimmy quickly put away his treasures, doing up the little buckle carefully and patting it affectionately.

The wind was like the day before, a strong easterly, almost dead astern, causing the ship to roll in the heavy sea.

The boys were still nauseous and Hughie was now bringing up almost pure blood. Too ill to work, he was allowed to return to the sail room.

As the day passed the weather worsened. Rain was lashing down in torrents and the Captain ordered the sail to be shortened. There was little that the boys could do on deck. Safety lines had been rigged and even the seasoned sailors looked ashen and moved cautiously about their business. All the boys, except Bryson, who was sent to the forecastle head, ostensibly to look out for other shipping, but really as a punishment, were given tasks inside the vessel.

John was in the forecastle, being shown how to tie a bowline by a sailor with bushy eyebrows.

"No, ye's gone wrong again." He undid the knot.

"Look, just lay the runnin' end across the line like this… aye that's it… now twist your wrist round like this… and ye make a loop in the standing part… aye that's it. Now take the end round the back o' the standin' end and back down the loop… yes that's it… now pull it tight… Very good! We'll make a sailor of ye yet. Now do it again but a bigger bight next time. Ye'd not fit a bairn in that one."

John practised the knot, his tongue sticking out of the corner of his mouth with concentration. After three or four successful attempts, he put the line of rope on his lap and looked thoughtful.

"Can I ask a question, Sir?"

"About the knot?"

"No, about the voyage. How much longer will it take?"

"Lord, we're hardly out o' British waters. It'll take three weeks or more an' if we catch the ice off Newfoundland it could take a few weeks longer'n that tae reach Quebec."

"Is it goin' tae be rough and rainin' all the way?"

"I don't know laddie. It certainly hasna started well. Ye coulda picked a better time for a trip."

"Will I stop bein' sick soon?"

"Ye will, but it could take a week or so. We're rollin a lot 'cause we're runnin' before. She always rolls when the wind's up her arse. A change o' wind direction will steady her, ye'll feel a wee bit better then. Have ye no coat?"

"Not here I haven't. I had tae leave it at home."

"I'll see what I can do. I can't promise nothin' mind. I think the weather's on the change. It may get colder."

A week of wet and rough weather passed. By the fifth day of the journey John, Brand, Reilly and Currie were feeling less sick and more willing to eat, but Bryson, Hughie and Jimmy were still unable to keep much down.

The boys' rations had remained ample for their normal needs since they had been discovered and those who couldn't eat were saving their rations to eat when things improved.

It was discovered by one of the seamen that mould was beginning to form on some of the sails stored in the sailroom. This was put down to condensation caused by the stowaways' wet clothes drying during the night. The mate was called to examine the sails and upon moving one, discovered the hidden store of biscuit, bread and vegetables. This was summarily confiscated. On this day the weather was better. It was not raining and an occasional patch of blue showed through threadbare grey cloud. All the stowaways were working on deck. Kerr walked forward in company with the boatswain.

"We're makin' too much leeway. Take in the fore to'gallant, see if that does it; if not we'll haul down the outer jib too. A tricky wind this…" His voice trailed off as he saw Bryson, who had been holystoning the deck, on hands and knees by the galley door. He was vomiting.

"Look at that, Lawrence. More good food wasted." He approached Bryson who was too preoccupied to notice.

"Look, beef! We give the brats beef! What a waste! He stood hard on Bryson's hand. "You won't vomit like that again in a hurry. I'll see the ground of your stomach before ye get any more beef on this ship."

Bryson clenched his teeth against the pain in his fingers and fought against the urge to cry out. This was not the time or place to retaliate. But soon, he thought. Soon.

That evening as darkness began to fall, all the tired stowaways except Bryson shuffled, heavy limbed, to the sailroom door. Reilly tried to open it.

"Why is it locked?" he asked.

"Are you sure it's locked?" said Brand, trying the door. Finding that it was, he went to the nearest sailor and asked where the key was kept.

"Ye'll have tae ask Mr Kerr for it, I can't give it tae ye."

Brand scanned the deck and saw the Mate standing with the helmsman on the poop. With trepidation he approached Kerr.

"Excuse me Sir…" he said politely, "the sailroom is locked and we can't get in. Can we have the key please?"

"Ye cannot. From now onwards ye can sleep in the fore hold, so take y'sels there."

"Why's that Sir?"

Kerr tilted his head back with disdain. "Because I say ye will."

"In the hold?" exclaimed Reilly when told. "In a pitch black hold, full of filthy coal and stinkin' oakum. Did youse smell the stench when they took the hatch covers off? Enough to knock a horse unconscious!"

The boys dragged themselves forward and one by one descended the ladder into the hold. Peter Currie held his nose and Jimmy McGinnes wrinkled his in reply.

Despite the hatch covers having been off for most of the day, the hold still stank. A dull yellow light came from a small Davy lamp fixed to one of the bulwark timbers.

"Well, here we are boys," exclaimed Reilly with outstretched arms and heavy irony, "welcome to the Palace of Arran."

John waited at the foot of the ladder for Hughie to descend.

"Alright?" he asked, peering at Hughie's top lit face, the light seeming to make the boy's eyes more sunken and haunted than they actually were.

"Aye" said Hughie dismissively, but aware of his friend's sincere concern.

Near the lamp were bales of oakum and bundles of coiled rope. The older stowaways were already arranging them to make the environment as comfortable as possible. A table had been made from a tightly coiled large diameter rope with a stiff tarpaulin folded over it. Smaller coils and bales of oakum were arranged around it for seating.

"Quite like home, is it not?" said Reilly.

"I'd hate tae live wi' you then" responded Brand.

"Oh, come on now, its perfect. All we need is a likeness of the mother in law on the wall to finish it off proper"

"You keep talkin' like that an' Kerr'll finish you off," said Brand.

Reilly rubbed his hands together. "Tis pretty filthy stuff though."

"All we need is somethin' tae eat at this splendid table of yours," said Brand.

"D'ye want me tae get ye somethin' tae eat?" said John to Hughie.

"I'd rather just sleep. I'm awful tired."

"Ye must keep eatin. Ye've hardly eaten anythin since…" Hughie interrupted.

"I canna help it. What's the point anyway, anything I do eat comes up again," he sighed. "Perhaps, if ye bring somethin' back wi' ye…"

Brand was at the head of the ladder and shouted down to those below. "I just caught a whiff of food cookin'. Smells gorgeous."

All except Hughie climbed the ladder to the deck and followed their noses to the galley. Reilly put his head round the open door.

"Five hungry persons, all present and correct Sir."

"You're not goin tae like this…" said the cook, who then gave them half a ship's biscuit each. "That's it – nothin' else, except for your pot o' coffee."

"You're jokin'! Come on now, we're hungry." said Brand.

"I'm starving," added John.

"It's nothin tae do wi' me," said the cook, defensively. "Mr Kerr has ordered that from now on ye's tae get nae more than half a biscuit daily. I have tae do as I'm told."

"I don't believe this. Why?" demanded Brand.

"Look, I just do as I'm told, I don't ask why."

"'Is this a joke? Tell me you're only jokin'," said Reilly.

"I wish I was," said the cook.

"What's goin' on? Why's he bein' so funny to us?" said John.

"I dunno," said Brand.

"I better go see him about it."

Brand had half an idea that the cook was joking and thought that the threat of going to the mate would end the nonsense. The half expected recall from the cook did not come and his purposeful stride took him to a seaman who was tidying the ropes around the mizzen pin rail.

"Where's Mr Kerr?" he asked.

"In his cabin, I expect."

Brand descended into the stern quarters and wondered which door was Kerr's. A gruff mumbling from the door to the right hand of the stairs gave the game away. The youth tried to calm himself and present a polite manner to the Mate. He knocked. The door opened and Brand was shocked to see Kerr very much the worst for drink. His eyes were glazed and his moustache and beard wet and spiky. He was in shirtsleeves and held a whisky bottle in one hand.

"Yes?" he slurred.

"Sorry tae disturb ye Sir, but we've only been given half a biscuit each for supper."

"Aye. So?"

"Well Sir, we usually have a cooked meal."

"Used to. Not usually. Used to. Ye better tighten your belts, it seems we've bin' givin' ye far too much grub. So much that ye were hidin' it in the sail room. Ye's all too fat and tired tae work well. There's nothin like a touch of hunger tae make a man work harder."

"I'm sorry Sir," said Brand indignantly, "we do work hard – all of us, even the wee ones, even Hughie McEwan, who's not very well at all."

"I'll be the judge o' whether ye's workin' hard enough!" spat Kerr, poking his finger hard into Brand's chest. "Now get out!"

"But that's unfair," said Brand.

The reply came unexpectedly. Kerr thrust his hand over Brand's face and forced him backwards out of the doorway. This sent the youth crashing against the wall of the cabin opposite.

"Get back in your black hole with the other brats! Any more of your nonsense and ye can starve!" He slammed the door.

Brand climbed the stairway and emerged stone-faced on the deck, where he was met by Reilly, John and McGinnes.

"Oh well, ye tried," said Reilly. "There's no talkin' to the man."

"He was stinkin' drunk," spat Brand, his eyes unusually wild. As the quartet sauntered listlessly forward to the hold he turned round and shouted, "He was stinkin' drunk!"

Upon their approach to the fore hatch, they could see the crouching figure of Bryson, silhouetted against the gloomy sky, still wearily scraping the deck and muttering to himself.

## 8. *Bryson seeks revenge*

At ten o' clock a sailor approached Bryson, who was still listlessly scraping the deck.

"Ye can stand down now" he said. Without any response other than a scowl Bryson made his way to the hatch and descended the ladder into the hold. Brand heard him coming. The others were asleep.

"I've saved ye somethin' tae eat," he said quietly. Bryson flopped down next to Brand and puffed irritably.

"Currie tells me Kerr's cut our rations," he said finally.

"Aye, half a biscuit each – that's all," said Brand.

"The bastard!"

"Aye, he is. I went to ask him about it. He was bloody pissed and went for me. He's a nasty piece of work. Oh, here's your biscuit."

Bryson took the biscuit and picked off a weevil. "Tae think I moaned about workin in Scott's sugar house. God, look at me now! It's only the thought o' gettin tae Quebec that's keepin me goin'. Ye can joke about it, but I'm goin' tae get that bastard – wait and see…"

Brand sighed. "Look, I've had some of his rough stuff too but…" he thought carefully before continuing, measuring his words as he spoke. "I know it would make ye feel better but I really don't think that havin' a go at him will solve anythin'.

It'll only make things worse." Brand threw a glance at the sleeping boys and lowered his voice to a whisper. "Think of the wee ones – think o' poor wee Hughie McEwan. He's not well now. If they make things worse for us it could kill him."

"Someone as feeble as him shouldn't have come. Anyway, it's a personal thing. When I've finished wi' Kerr he won't be able tae take revenge on us."

"You know that would be mutiny. You could hang for it."

"How can it be mutiny? I'm not one of the crew."

"Ye don't have tae be. At best ye'd be sent tae prison."

"I'll take my chance. Prison don't frighten me none, I've already bin' there an' it's no worse than this existence."

This news shocked Brand. "Ye've been tae prison?"

"Aye…" his tone was defensive.

"What for?"

"None of your business." Bryson's tone was firm, precluding any further probing.

"Are ye lookin' forward tae gettin' tae Quebec?" There was no answer, but Brand kept talking. "I am. I did some engineerin' at the sawmill, ye know, maintainin' the machines, doin' repairs and suchlike. I reckon there'll be a need for skills like that. I'll have the chance tae make somethin' o' mysel'."

"Aye," responded Bryson without enthusiasm.

"What d'ye plan tae do when we get there?"

"Dunno. Somethin'. Dunno."

Undeterred by Bryson's disinterest, Brand continued. "It's a big country, wide open. Everythin's growin' wi opportunity an' fortunes tae be made wi a bit o' luck an' hard work. There was a man who lived in East Quay Lane. He stowed away like us. He was away nae more than a couple o' years an' comes back a real swell, wi' enough tae buy the yard where his Pa worked. He was poor an' nae cleverer than ye or me an…"

Bryson had finished his biscuit and lay down, interrupting Brand.

"Look," he said irritably, "I been workin for fifteen hours, my fingers are raw, I ache all over an' I'm tired. Will ye shut up now? I want tae go tae sleep."

Brand shrugged his shoulders, lay down and looked at the dimly-lit forms of John and Hughie sleeping on the oakum. He knew how tired and hungry he felt, despite getting tidbits from the galley. How hungry they must be with nothing other than the half biscuit.

All the stowaways' 'Greenock grey' complexions had been blasted by the bite of the wind and the scour of sea spray to a new, healthy ruddiness. All that is, except for Hughie. The hint of redness on his cheeks and nose only served to emphasise the deathly pallor of the rest of his face. The very skin of his face seemed stretched and lined and every day he looked older.

The motion of the ship seemed to Brand to have eased. Although tired, he couldn't sleep and decided to go on deck. Picking his way past the sleeping stowaways, he took up his jacket and climbed the ladder.

The wind was cold but less biting than before, yet it still had enough sting to make his eyes water. He turned up his collar and leaned on the rail, looking out to sea. The cloud blanket was broken and the moonlight sculpted its tattered form with eerie phosphorescent light. As the clouds moved, the moon cast beams on to the sea, jewelling it with light. It was beautiful.

Brand looked around. Endless sea and here he was, trapped on this small wooden island miles from anywhere. He wondered how his family were. Three years in the sawmill with his father had been more than enough. He saw in his father what he would become if he didn't break away. Although he had graduated away from the mundane cutting of timber, to the repair and maintenance of the machines, all that lay ahead was a life of near poverty, eking out a living, while the mill owner grew fat on his sweat. He'd probably meet a local girl, already there were some who had showed interest, get married and the cycle would continue. He was bright and had done well at school. The railway was beginning to push westward across America. He was fit and had always made friends easily. Perhaps he could get a job as an engineer – they must need engineers – and work his way up. Perhaps.. An unexpected voice behind him made him start. It was Reilly.

"What are you doin' out here?" said the Irishman.

"God, you made me jump," replied Brand.

"Sorry," said Reilly with a smile in his voice. He joined Brand at the rail. "Weather seems to be gettin' quieter"

"Mm…" responded Brand. "Still cold though. Could get even colder, so one of the sailors said, there's usually icebergs off Newfoundland."

"At least the ship's not rollin' so much. You feelin' better?"

"Oh, on and off. I feel a bit queasy now and again. Haven't been sick for a while though."

" Have ye family in Quebec?" asked Brand.

"No…" Reilly paused. "I have no family; none that I know of anyway. My mother and father died during the famine. I was brought up in the workhouse. The Master and Matron and a few hundred other poor souls are the only family I know. I've got a couple of friends in Nova Scotia… but I may go to America… see what's about."

"I'm goin tae try for a job as an engineer or perhaps a clerk on the railway."

"Ye can write?"

"Aye," said Brand, with a hint of pride in his voice, "and read and do figures. Y'need figures for engineerin'."

"School wasn't up to much, y'might say, at the workhouse. I can write me name but not much else, but I'm good wi' me hands and I learn quick."

Brand looked out to sea and smiled. "A few weeks and we'll see land on that horizon. The land of opportunity, they call it."

"I hope it is, Davie boy, I really do," said Reilly wistfully.

They became silent for a while, each with his own thoughts focused on the horizon, that sharp, insistent line that seemed so static, despite the evidence of the ship's wake.

Finally Brand spoke. "Did ye come straight tae Scotland from Ireland?"

"No, I was a while in England, lookin' for work, but as soon as they heard my accent I was either told to bugger off or was offered work, at half the pay of an Englishman."

"Why was that?"

"They said that we only work half as hard as the English. T'wasn't true, but there were so many o'us lookin' for work. I had the choice – take it or starve. After a while I had to get away, so I came to Greenock, hopin' for work in the shipyards. T'was the same story there. The Irish aren't welcome."

"There's lots of Irish in Greenock"

"I know, we can starve anywhere, just look for a gutter and you'll see an Irishman livin' in it." There was bitterness in his voice. He watched his fingers toying with droplets of water on the rail.

"I'm sorry Davie, I'm goin' on a bit."

"Ye've just had bad luck. Ye've a nice way about ye," said Brand cheerfully. "Ye'll do well in the New World. I'd say your chances are a lot better than Bryson's."

"Jesus, that lad's an idiot. He'd make a fight out o' sayin' good mornin'!"

"He still says he's goin to get Kerr, y'know."

"He's a fool if he does. We'll all be hangin' from the yard arm before he's finished."

"Ye can't reason with him," said Brand. "He just gets tetchy."

"I shouldn't bother – save your breath. God I'm starvin'! I shall be eatin' the coal before long. I'm twenty two, an' gettin the same ration as little Johnnie Paul, who must be all of ten!"

"He's twelve, not ten."

"Twelve? Never! Jesus, he's a small chap."

"McEwan's the youngest, he's just eleven."

"McEwan, now there's a sickly soul. He's havin' a rough time of it. Have you heard him coughin'?"

"No."

"Well, you listen tonight. He's not coughin' fierce but he's coughin' more'n he used to. Consumption I reckon. I've seen enough o'it to know the signs."

They fell into a gloomy silence. Brand looked up at the sails which, lit brightly by the moonlight, were now flapping slackly. "Wind's still droppin'," he said.

"Quite a nice change. Anyway, I'm for bed – back to the stinkin' hole, eh?"

"I'll stay up a while," said Reilly.

As Brand crossed the deck he heard the familiar voice of Kerr ordering the trimming of the sails, and as he approached the hold he thought he saw a shadow move near the fore pin rail, but upon looking again it had gone. He went below and lay down, looking around at the others, who were asleep. He listened to their steady breathing and suddenly realised that Bryson was not among them.

Reilly was still on deck but as the crew came forward to man the fore windlass he was concerned that he would be ordered to help and so took refuge behind the forecastle companionway roof. Kerr's voice came from the port side of the ship. Reilly peered around the edge of the curved roof to see where he was.

As the Mate came past the fore deckhouse a figure, wielding a belaying pin, lunged at him. Kerr parried the blow and using the speed and weight of the youth, swung him hard against the ship's rail. Immediately Kerr laid into him with both fists.

The belaying pin clattered harmlessly along the deck. It was now Bryson who had to defend himself, but he was powerless against the mate's raining blows. A few more punches to the stomach and Bryson doubled up, falling into the gulley near to a freeing port.

Kerr first kicked, then pushed the now cringing and pleading youth towards the port in the bulwark. Bryson moved and fell with his back against the top hung flap of the port. Under his weight, it swung open. The Mate forced his victim's head and shoulder through the opening. Bryson clung desperately to its sides, despite the kicks and blows. He could see and hear the cold black water below him, foamed by the ship's swift passage. Once in the sea, his life would be measured in minutes.

Kerr kicked Bryson's hand from the side of the opening. The youth's other shoulder was now through the port, the bottom edge of which was digging into the small of his back. Bryson's fingers were now clutching the edges of the port, while the heavy steel flap forced his head backwards. The mate's constant pushing and kicking was inching him out.

Reilly could remain in his hiding place no longer.

"No!" he shouted, "Stop! No!" He ran up to the Mate, pulling him back. Bryson lost no time in scrambling back into safety and away from the port. Kerr pushed Reilly away, stood up and sauntered towards his victim and, despite his cries of 'No, No,' gave the youth another hefty kick. Bryson groaned.

The Mate looked at Reilly, who became fearful for his own safety, but now there were some other seamen looking on. Kerr retrieved his cap from the deck, put it on and spoke quietly to Bryson.

"Any time laddie. Any time. I'll be lookin' out for ye. Next time, ye'll hang!" Brushing his sleeves with his hands, he walked slowly off. Reilly helped the sobbing and winded Bryson to his feet.

"He was goin' tae kill me. He was goin' tae throw me overboard!" His lip was split and bleeding, there was a small cut on his cheek and his forehead was grazed where it had grated against the rough paint of the freeing port flap. It was then that Brand came up.

"What's the commotion about?" He saw Bryson's injuries. "What's happened tae him?"

"The Mate's given him a good seein' to."

"What for?"

"It was his own fault, he attacked Kerr."

"No I didn't!" he protested.

"You did, I saw you," said Reilly.

"I told you to keep away from him, didn't I?" said Brand.

"Bloody idiot! Now we'll all suffer for it." Between them they helped Bryson below into the hold.

## 9.   John gets a coat – and a haircut

A shout from the Boatswain aroused the stowaways.

"Come on, it's four o' clock!" With moans and groans they stirred themselves. Hughie coughed a little and Bryson, with good reason, groaned more than anyone.

"What's happened tae you?" asked John.

"I was beaten up by Kerr," grumbled Bryson, hunched and clutching his bruised ribs.

"You're bigger than him."

"I was held down by the crew," he said quietly, hoping that Brand and Reilly wouldn't hear.

"No ye weren't," said Brand, still angry, "He was better than you – made ye look like a big girl! No Johnnie, he went for Kerr like we told him not to, and Kerr knocked the stuffing out of him. He didn't need any help."

"He winded me. I'd ha' done for him if I hadna been winded. I'll get him next time though, you wait and see."

"Oh grow up Bryson," said Brand crossly, "Ye heard what he said, next time ye'll hang."

"Is that what he said?" asked John in amazement.

"Sure it is," said Reilly. "You try that again Bryson and I'll help him push ye overboard!"

It was with a strong sense of foreboding that the eldest three stowaways climbed the ladder to the deck. The four boys followed on. The Boatswain was waiting by the fore pin rail as they emerged. He directed them to their duties for the day. Nothing was said about the previous night. The moon still gave out its light and the sea breathed lightly in shallow silver rhythms, diffused by the mist. The dark sails hung limply from their yards as if asleep.

As crimson stained the eastern horizon smoke began drifting from the galley chimney, signalling the preparation of breakfast. John and Hughie were on top of the rear deckhouse, scraping paint from one of the boats. The burgoo that was being cooked smelled wonderful. John could contain himself no longer. Climbing down he went to the galley and put his head around the open door. William Salton, the cook, was stirring the steaming mixture.

"Please can we have some breakfast sir? We're starvin'."

Salton sighed. "I can't gi' ye nothin'. Mr Kerr tells me when tae feed ye. I have tae do as I'm told."

"Just a little, He'd never know," said John, putting on the appealing face that had melted the heart of his mother when he wanted his own way. Much to his surprise it worked.

"Look, ye'll have tae bide a while. I canna gi'ye any o' this, but if ye wait until the Captain and Mate are at breakfast, come round tae the pantry window on the poop just after eight an' I'll see if I can find ye somethin'. Ye must take it down in the hold tae eat it. Some o' the crew might report ye, then I'm for it. But come quietly for the grub, the officers will be next door in the saloon."

As the sun rose it burned off the thin mist to reveal a calm sea and a blue mackerel sky with high cirrus cloud. The sun shone and took the chill off the morning air.

The Second Mate, Mr Niven, had ordered the suite of sails to be changed. The heavy-weather sails were one-by-one replaced by the thinner and lighter fair-weather sails. This done, there was still little wind to fill them, despite all sail possible being set.

The crewmembers took the opportunity to catch up on their washing. Lines were rigged from the shrouds to the masts and the washing was hung to dry. All this looked quite festive and the change of weather seemed to have brought about a convivial atmosphere among the sailors.

Just before eight John left his work and, carrying a bucket, sauntered as casually as he could to the poop of the vessel. He crept along to the pantry. The porthole was open, allowing a warm, scented aroma of food to escape, and he could see the cook inside, stirring the ashes of the stove with a poker.

"Psst…" he hissed.

Salton didn't hear him, so he waited for the clatter by the stove to sibside.

"Psst…" he repeated, a little louder.

Salton passed a paper wrapped package up to him and whispered, "Take it below mind, don't tell anyone else and don't get caught."

John casually dropped the package in the bucket and walked back to the deckhouse, whistling nonchalantly. He whispered to Hughie to come with him.

Knowing that the bucket contained food he was keen to comply. "What ye got?"

"Ssh… Dunno. Come below," whispered John. In the hold John opened up the paper to reveal pieces of beef, bacon, bread and broken pieces of biscuit. They pounced on the food like pirates on treasure and in seconds it had gone.

"Don't tell the others," said John, screwing up the paper into a ball and throwing into the darkness of the hold.

A minute or two later they regained the deck and walked back to their work. Niven stopped them.

"Where've ye been?"

"We've been tae the toilet," answered Hughie.

"Ye must ask tae go. I can't have ye skivin' off every five minutes."

"No Sir," said John. Quietly giggling the boys went back to their work. They had hardly started when the sailor, who had taught John to tie knots, came up.

"Here," he said, "It'll be too big for ye but it'll be warm." He produced a thick velour coat of bright blue. "Try it on."

It was not a large size, but on the boy's small frame it seemed so. John rolled up the cuffs so that his hands could be seen.

"Not bad eh?" said the sailor.

"Thank ye sir," said John joyfully, his hands smoothing the soft material. It may have been a little faded and stained but already he could feel its warmth. Over his arm the sailor had other clothes, which were obviously too large for the small boys. He gave both Brand and Reilly a shirt and pair of trousers each.

The appearance of Kerr and the Captain on deck sent a needle of fear through the stowaways. The two men were engaged in what appeared to be a light-hearted conversation. As they approached the aft deckhouse Kerr looked up at the two boys, diligently scraping flakes of paint from the boat's gunwale.

"Ha, look at this Cap'n. That's a nice quiet coat ye've got there, laddie. There's no fear o' runnin' aboard another ship wi' ye on deck – as good as a lighthouse. Peacock blue eh? Ha, yes, Peacock Paul. Right Peacock?" They laughed. "An the other one dressed as grey as a clerk, like a telegraph boy. They're an odd couple aren't they – the peacock an' the telegraph boy." The two men enjoyed the joke and walked on much to John's and Hughie's relief.

So far only Davie Brand, Barney Reilly and occasionally Peter Currie had bothered to wash themselves. The filthy conditions in the hold had made all the stowaways quite dirty. The gift to Brand and Reilly of a further set of clothes meant that at last they could change and wash those they had worn since coming on board the Arran. Currie had brought a change of clothes with him but he had not bothered to wash them and both sets were grubby.

A message came from the Mate for the stowaways to assemble on the foredeck.

Kerr stood on the forecastle head with his elbows on the rail. When they were all there he stood erect and with a serious expression silently looked them up and down. The boys all wondered what was to come.

"I have been more than twenty years at sea. I have had tae suffer stowaways on many voyages, but in all my time I have never had the misfortune tae meet such a miserable bunch o' brats as you. Ye're filthy and probably lousy too. From now on

I want tae see a change in ye. I want ye tae keep y'sels clean an we'll start now. Who of ye has only one set o' clothes?"

Bryson, John, Hughie and Jimmy put their hands up.

He looked at Currie. "Have you got spare clothes?"

"Aye sir," he replied quietly.

"Well, get 'em now." Currie trotted off. "The rest of ye…" he continued, "strip off an' gi' your shirts, vests and trousers tae Brand."

The small boys did as they were told and stood naked, hunched and goose pimpled in the cold air. Bryson, however, was reluctant.

"C'mon Bryson," said Kerr, "Get your clothes off."

"I don't want to."

"D'ye want a good hidin'?"

"No." Kerr motioned that he expected more. "No Sir," said the youth submissively, beginning slowly to undress. When naked he stood, embarrassed, with head bowed and hands clasped loosely in front of his genitals. The bruises sustained during his fight with the mate could clearly be seen. After a few seconds, he looked up at Kerr, who made a point of looking him up and down and smirking. There was a cold superiority in his glare, which made Bryson afraid that there was more humiliation and violence to come.

The stowaways gasped as crew members threw buckets of seawater over their naked bodies. Hughie was off balance when his bucketful hit home and he fell over. They were all given a lump of hard yellow soap to wash themselves with.

"Do a proper job or I'll have ye scrubbed," said the Mate.

Although this statement was a general one, his eyes were firmly fixed on Bryson. Brand was ordered to wash and peg out the clothes, while Reilly was given a pair of heavy scissors and a brown jar containing a strange blue ointment.

"When they're clean, I want their hair cut to the scalp and this ointment put on their heads. It's tae kill the lice," said Kerr to Reilly.

"Aye Sir!" He opened the jar to smell it and quickly recoiled. "Jesus! That could bring tears to a glass eye."

Further buckets of water were poured over the boys to rinse away the thin lather. Kerr reached into his pocket, pulled out a short length of coiled rope and descended the steps from the forecastle head purposefully. John watched him approach Bryson, who was washing his head and neck, his eyes tightly shut against the sting of the lather and oblivious to the Mate's approach. Kerr allowed the coils of rope to drop and he swung the rope back and forth gently as if testing it. Slowly he took the rope behind him and judged its trajectory, suddenly, with all his might, lashed Bryson's buttocks. The youth leapt forward, screaming in pain.

"Get a move on, put some energy into it!"

Bryson, clearly frightened, quickly complied.

"That's more like it," smiled Kerr.

John and the other boys doubled their efforts in fear of similar treatment. By the time that they had finished, they were all blotchily pink, clean and shivering uncontrollably.

A barrel was placed in the centre of the deck and first Bryson, then Hughie, Jimmy McGinnes and John sat and had their hair shorn to the scalp.

The small boys laughed at one another as Reilly applied the potent blue ointment to their uneven stubbly tufts of hair. McGinnes complained that it made his head sting. They were then instructed to run around the deck to dry themselves and get warm. Kerr stood by the rail idly swinging his rope, encouraging them to run faster. Each time Bryson came by, he feinted at him with the rope and the youth flinched to avoid the lash that didn't come. Kerr laughed out loud at his humiliation.

By the second circuit of the deck, Hughie was very tired and had begun a coughing fit, during which he brought up blood. He sat down on the main hatch, fighting for breath. Kerr had noticed his absence from the runners and came to find him. Upon seeing him approach, he again staggered into a run. Kerr put his arm out and stopped the boy.

"Get your coat and go below," he said. Hughie was only too keen to oblige.

The stench of the hold seemed even more pungent after the clean smell of the soap. The boy sat on a bale of oakum and tried to consciously control the pounding in his head and heart. Another sharp coughing fit seemed, for the moment, to clear his chest. When he had recovered from his efforts he felt a little better than he had done for the past couple of days. He was clean and refreshed, the food had been welcome and it was good not to feel sick, and to see the sunshine. Wrapped in his coat, Hughie laid down and drifted off to sleep.

When he awoke, it was to the sound of music. He wondered if it was a dream, but no, he could definitely hear music.

## 10. Prelude to a storm

Hughie was surprised to find that his clean and dry clothes had been brought down to him while he was asleep. He dressed quickly and climbed the ladder. Peering over the hatch, he could see people grouped around the main hold.

Some of the main hatch covers remained in place and a seaman was dancing a hornpipe to the accompaniment of a concertina played by the sailor with bad teeth. The ship was almost becalmed and work had come to a halt. All save the helmsman seemed to be there.

Washing criss-crossed the deck and its gentle fluttering in the sun added to the relaxed carnival atmosphere of the occasion. The dance finished and Kerr spoke – his face was flushed and he slurred his words:

"Jeremiah, gi' us 'Waitin' for the Day'."

"Ah, yes…" Jeremiah played a chord and launched into a jolly rhythm. He began:

> *"The worst old brig that ever did weigh,*
> *sailed out of Greenock on a windy day…"*

Hughie was amazed at the beauty and clarity of his strong tenor voice. He found it hard to believe that such a wonderful sound could be produced from a mouth so diseased. The chorus came and the audience joined in:

> *"And we're waitin' for the day, waitin' for the day,*
> *waitin' for the day when we get our pay."*

All nine verses and choruses were sung and when the song ended, the applause and cheers rang out across the empty ocean.

"As we've got some boys on board, who should be at school..." said Jeremiah smiling hideously, "I think we should educate them with 'The Sailor's Alphabet'."

The assembly cheered and John and Hughie exchanged smiles. Jimmy and Peter Currie were giggling. Hughie looked over to Bryson who was standing on the far side of the ship from Kerr. Even he was smiling.

A chord again signalled the key. Jeremiah threw back his head and began:

> "A is the anchor that hangs o'er the bow,
> B is the bowsprit that bends like a bow.
> C is the capstan we merrily heave round, and
> D is the davits we lower our boats down."

As one, all except the stowaways, who didn't know the song, joined in the chorus:

> "So merrily – so merrily – so merrily are we,
> There's no man on earth like a sailor at sea.
> Blow high or blow low – as the ship sails along,
> Give the sailor his grog and there's nothing goes wrong..."

When the last chorus and its applause finished, Jeremiah invited others to sing a song. There were no volunteers.

"Come on someone ... Hey you, Irish, the Irish are always singin'. Ye must have a song."

Reilly at first shook his head, embarrassed, but to cries of 'Go on!' from all sides, gave in and walked over to sit by Jeremiah.

Unlike the former songs, this one was a lament about the failure of the potato crop. There seemed real emotion in his voice, although it could have been nervousness.

He began quietly.

*"Oh, the praties they are small, over here, over here*
*Oh, the praties they are small, over here."*

His voice strengthened.

*"Oh, the praties they are small and we dig them in the fall,*
*and we eat them coats and all over here, over here."*

The thin reedy tone of Jeremiah's concertina reflected the plaintive quality of the song. Reilly continued.

*"Oh, I wish that we were geese, night and morn, night and morn,*
*Oh, I wish that we were geese, night and morn.*
*Oh, I wish that we were geese, we could live and die in peace,*
*'til the day of our decease, eatin, corn, eatin' corn."*

The final verse was sung with almost an evangelistic fervour:

*"Oh, we're ground down in the dust, over here, over here.*
*Oh, we're ground down in the dust, over here.*
*Oh, we're ground down in the dust, but the party that we trust,*
*will yet give us crumb for crust, over here, over here!"*

Its end was signalled by silence – a kind of reverence, which allowed the song some space for its emotion to disperse over the endless sea. The silence was broken by Kerr, who started clapping. He was joined by a rippling fusillade of applause and cheers. Reilly returned to the audience.

"Thank ye, Irish," said Jeremiah. "A powerful song, but a wee bit gloomy. How's about a hornpipe tae cheer us all up?"

Jeremiah launched into a fast and furious tune, which soon had all the audience clapping. A sailor came forward, jumped on to the hatch cover and danced with great skill. Each difficult manoeuvre was greeted with cheers as the tune began to speed up.

John so enjoyed the dancing that he began to join in.

"Come on Hughie, dance wi' me." Without giving his friend time to decline, He linked arms with the boy and swung him around. Currie and Jimmy soon got drawn into the dance, to the cheers of the crew.

What they lacked in skill was more than made up for by their enthusiasm. The hornpipe dancer encouraged them on to the hatch cover and they all danced and whirled to Jeremiah's concertina, creating gales of laughter and applause. At one point, Jimmy let go at the wrong time and was catapulted off the hatch. This induced a spontaneous roar of helpless laughter from the audience, many of whom were staggering and rolling about in their mirth.

Jeremiah was sweating as the music got faster and faster until finally the dancer was caught off balance and fell over, causing everyone else to do the same. The hatch cover was a mass of arms and legs all waving about helplessly.

The end was greeted with cheers and whistles that could almost have been heard back in Greenock.

When the noise had died down Kerr stood on the hatch.

"I want tae sing one now."

The company cheered.

"I want tae sing 'The Wreck o' the Vixen'."

The cheers died away. It was noticeable that the Captain left the audience.

"The Wreck o' the Vixen?" queried Jeremiah, looking a little concerned. "Wouldn't ye rather sing somethin' else?"

Kerr waved his arms about in emphasis.

"If I say I want tae sing 'The Wreck o' the Vixen', I want tae sing it!"

"But it's bad luck tae sing o' a wreck," said a sailor.

"What are ye? A bunch o' superstitious fishwives? Play it Jeremiah!"

The musician cast an unhappy glance to a sailor and played the introductory chords stiffly.

"He'll do for us all," muttered the sailor behind John, crossing himself. He's temptin' the devil."

Kerr began singing in a deep uncultured voice. The tune, itself having a mood of menace, filled the company with dread.

*"I must go, I said to Mary, I must go away tae sea.*
*For I must earn a fortune fast, so that I can marry thee.*
*When I reached the dock at Greenock,*
    *only one ship needed crew,*
*That was the brig 'The Vixen', she seemed good ship and true."*

The chorus began:

*"Away my boys, for Baltimore, we'll sail the salt seas o'er…"*

Kerr stopped singing.

"Come on you bastards!" he spat. "Join in wi' the chorus… I'll do it again."

*Away my boys, for Baltimore, we'll sail the salt seas o'er,*

*And when this trip is finished, I'll sail the sea nae more,
But return tae home in Gourock, gold and silver in my hand
And I'll wed my darlin' Mary and farm no other's land."*

Kerr was supported in the chorus more by mumbling than singing and in successive choruses even this petered out. He carried on.

*"Oh, do not go, said Mary I want ye here wi' me,
I do not need, before we're wed, tae be widowed by the sea.
I want land that is my own, said I and will be no man's slave,
I'd rather die upon the sea than go a pauper tae my grave."*

The dire song ground on. Kerr stood, determined in voice and posture, despite mutterings among the seamen. As the song progressed, some crew members slipped away from the audience, hoping that Kerr wouldn't notice. Sharp intakes of breath here and there and a flurry of arms making the sign of the cross ran through the assembly as the last two verses unfolded.

*"The storm it hit us hard as rocks
        and she shook from stern tae stem.
Our bow drove down to the sea's hard floor
        and then came up again.
The wind took off our forecourse,
        and then the mainmast too,
and when the main hatch cover failed,
        I knew that we were through..."*

The final chorus was greeted with silence. Jeremiah's eyes showed fear, but Kerr was oblivious and launched into the final verse. His lips, wet and red, literally spat out the final verse. As he began it, a small cloud obscured the sun, creating a sudden chill to the air. His dark eyes glowed with a fire to tempt the devil. Some saw the devil in them.

"The Vixen sank wi' all hands lost, she went down wi'out a trace
Now I'll never again see my own true love
        no more see her dear sweet face.
If I had listened to her good sense
        I'd not be drowning in the sea,
It was only stubborn greediness that made an end o' me."

The last line of the song was greeted with silence.

"Come on! All my hard work! Gi' me a hand!" Kerr began clapping himself; a thin ripple of applause joined in.

Kerr stepped down from the hatch.

"One more tae finish off then," he said, irritably.

"Aye Sir," said Jeremiah, desperate to kill the mood of fear and gloom. His eyes sparkled as he played a little riff on his concertina.

"You little ones shouldn'a listen tae this. It's a song I learned from an Englishman" (there were boos from some of the audience) "But I'm still goin tae do it." He began.

"While cruisin' round Yarmouth one day for a spree,
I met a fair damsel the wind blowin' free,
I'm a fast goin' clipper – my kind sir, said she,
I'm ready for cargo – my hold it is free..."

The song was acted out by Jeremiah who sang in falsetto for the woman's part and in a lecherous voice for the sailor's. The audience responded with laughter and lewd noises at the appropriate parts of the song.

When the noise of the applause had died, the crew members dispersed. Only Jeremiah and a few others who were off watch remained, but the frivolity and bawdiness of the last song had failed to obliterate the mood created by Kerr's song.

Back in their position on the roof of the after deckhouse, John and Hughie continued scraping the flaking paint from the gunwale of the boat. John looked out to the horizon.

"Land!" he exclaimed, standing up. Hughie stood up too.

"Oh yes, there on the horizon. I can see it too. Is it America?"

"Don't know," said John.

"Land it's not," said a sailor, climbing aloft. "That's cloud."

"Looks like land," said Hughie.

"Looks more like land than clouds. It's got hills," muttered John.

While they worked they watched the 'land' get nearer, coming towards the ship off the starboard bow. As it grew closer, the wind increased. The studding sails were taken in and the ship began to make good headway.

The 'land' was, as the sailor had said, cloud. It was thick and dark in colour. Again, one by one the sails were changed for the heavier set. For the first time both Reilly and Brand were sent aloft to help in the setting of the sails. Neither wanted to go, but their fear of the Mate's wrath was greater than their fear of falling from the masts.

They climbed the shrouds slowly and deliberately, fear stiffening their movements. Once they had gained the relative safety of the 'top' they were reluctant to move out on to the yards on the footropes, so were allowed to remain on the top to haul on various lines of rope.

John and Hughie peered up at them periodically. They looked uncomfortably stiff and clung with one hand to the shrouds to the cross tree above.

The wind continued to gust and the ship began to heel over alarmingly as the cloud crawled darkly toward them. The sea beneath it was black in colour. The coming of night was hastened by the dark cloud rolling over the masthead of the ship. The blocking out of the sun brought an unwelcome chill to the air. Kerr was on deck, in serious discussion with Captain Watt and the boatswain.

Farthing-sized dark stains speckled the deck and sails as the rain began. Sailors appeared in oilskins and before long the rain was so heavy that the bow of the Arran could hardly be made out. It ran like beaded curtains from the foot of the sails. The two boys took refuge under the upturned boat and John watched the ice cold water eddying around his red toes, on its way to the deck.

A momentary flash in the distance heralded a rumble of thunder. Kerr ordered the sail to be shortened. The royals, topgallants and upper topsails were clewed up, flapping noisily as they spilled the air. Crew members, silhouetted against the bruised sky, moved out along the yards to do battle with the sodden, flapping canvas.

By this time both Brand and Reilly, still aloft, were past work and just stood clinging to the shrouds. All the time the sea and wind were increasing. Encouraged by other crewmembers who had also finished their work aloft, they came down to the deck. Pale and shaking, they were patted on the back by the sailors for their efforts. They were sent down to the hold to join the other stowaways. The carpenter was waiting, mallet in hand. As Brand and Reilly descended the ladder, the hatch covers were put in place, the canvas overlaid and pinned down with battens.

The blows as the carpenter banged in the wedges resounded like a drum through the hold.

"It's like being nailed in a coffin," said Reilly, echoing all their thoughts.

The Arran's bow suddenly dipped and a cask fell from the half-deck onto the coal, splitting open and spilling its contents of meal. The bow's descent was halted abruptly to a scrunching sound. Shuddering, it rose again, creaking loudly, before again plunging steeply. The boys felt that they were being pulled down to the bottom of the ocean. John and Hughie clung together in fear and the ominous words of Kerr's song could not be driven from John's mind.

*"Our bow drove down to the sea's hard floor..."*

The sickly yellow light from the Davy lamp dimmed so that only vague shapes could be seen. Finally, the lamp went out. The hold was now in pitch blackness. A sudden skidding noise followed by a bang in the hold made John clutch Hughie's hand all the harder. Something else had fallen from the half deck.

"Christ Almighty!" said Brand.

"Jesus! What was that?" said Reilly simultaneously. John could imagine him crossing himself.

After a half hour of buffeting in the black hold, with only their own physical sensations for company, all the stowaways began to feel sick. Before long the sound of vomiting accompanied the crash and bang of the storm.

The nausea, combined with the violently irregular motion of the Arran, induced a feeling bordering on panic in those in the sealed, dark hold. All the stowaways were huddled together. Currie and Jimmy were clasping Brand's arm. He could feel their trembling.

A clap of thunder shook the vessel and produced a gasp from all the stowaways. Water could be heard slamming against the hatch covers and rushing around the coamings above their heads.

Suddenly Hughie felt a sprinkling of water hit his face. He tasted its saltiness.

"Oh, Lord save us, water's comin' in!" The song again leapt into John's mind.

> *"The wind took away our forecourse*
> *and then the mainmast too,*
> *And when the main hatch cover failed,*
> *I knew that we were through."*

An atmosphere of blind fear prevailed. Hughie and John gasped with terror at every sudden movement or noise of the ship's seemingly uncontrolled career. They were now tightly clinging together, periodically sobbing. They listened the sounds of the storm. Any new sound would strike terror into their hearts. The overall noise was deafening.

The rigging screamed as the wind tore at it, and the timbers creaked, cracked, groaned and shuddered in their battle with the storm. What was happening above could only be imagined by those in their black prison.

When the Arran heeled sharply John was sure that a capsize was imminent. He tried to put it from his mind but couldn't. They would go down with the ship – there was no way of getting out.

> "And when the main hatch cover failed,
> I knew that we were through."

In his mind he heard the crew muttering about the devil, and saw Kerr as the devil incarnate, having brought the storm on by witchcraft. Witchcraft that would send the Arran to the same fate as the 'Vixen'.

As the turbulence carried on hour after hour, a kind of numb resignation took the place of terror. John tried to judge each crash, each violent movement, against the one that had preceded it, to assess if the storm was growing or slackening in intensity. John and Hughie had both been sick and Hughie could taste blood when his vomiting induced a coughing fit. The storm gradually abated and the boys fell into a thankful, exhausted sleep.

John woke to the sound of the wedges being knocked out above. As a section of hatch cover was removed, a shaft of bright light penetrated the darkness. The greatcoated figure of Kerr descended the ladder, followed by a seaman. The stowaways stood up.

"Ugh, what a stink. Why's the lamp out?" He removed it from the bulwark and shook it.

"Empty. Get it filled and lit will ye."

The seaman took it and climbed the ladder.

"A rough time for ye yesterday. Ye didn't have tae work much though did ye? Well, today's different. I expect ye tae work twice as hard as ye've had a wee rest."

He looked at Bryson whose head was turned away.

"You listenin' Bryson?"

"Aye," mumbled the youth.

"Aye what? Do I have tae teach ye manners?"

"Aye *Sir*," replied Bryson, betraying anxiety.

"Ye can start by cleanin' up your vomit and makin' the hold shipshape. When you've done I'll have a look, an' if it's done good enough, ye can have somethin' tae eat. I want this place smellin like Well Park in the spring. D'ye understand Bryson?"

"Aye Sir."

"If it's not done properly ye'll keep doin' it 'til it is. I don't want any water used. The cargo has tae be kept dry. Remember that. We don't want a fire. There's no fire office out here."

The sailor returned with the lamp, which was reinstated in the bulwark. By its light he could see the two barrels which had fallen from the half deck in the storm. One of them was still intact.

Kerr pointed.

"That barrel can go back up to the 'tween deck – see to it Reilly, I'll throw down some buckets for the rest o'ye."

"Sure he reminds me o' the mother I never had," said Reilly when he had gone. "All heart."

## 11. *The cold bites*

As soon as the tarpaulin cover had been flicked back over the hatch, the stowaways, as one, pounced on the meal from the broken barrel. Much of it had fallen through the coal, but enough remained to at least partially satisfy the boys' hunger. John, Hughie and Jimmy dissolved into gales of laughter at the sight of each other with their blue hair and blackened mouths where coal dust had accumulated. The older stowaways smiled.

Their work below completed, they sent Currie to inform the Mate. He scanned the coal with a critical eye, made Bryson scrape some pieces of coal clean and then took hold of Jimmy McGinnes' face, squeezing his cheeks so that his mouth pouted.

"What's all this round your mouth, laddie?"

"Nothin'," said the boy, as best as he could, his face still in the Mate's grip.

Kerr pushed the boy back on to the coal.

"Don't lie tae me. Ye've eaten the meal between ye, haven't ye?"

"It would only have been thrown away," said Reilly.

"Aye, it would. It wasn't even fit for pigs. So, really you've done me a favour – as you've already eaten you won't need anythin' from me. Right, let's have ye on deck, plenty o'work tae do."

As soon as John's head poked above the hatch coaming, the sleet in the cold wind stung his face. 'Still' he thought, 'I've a nice warm coat now.' When he had been on deck a while the warmth of the coat only seemed to emphasise the coldness of other parts of his body. He was particularly aware of his shorn head and of his bare feet on the wet, slippery deck.

Hughie was sent to carry on with scraping paint from the ship's boat while John and Jimmy were told to scrub the poop with deck brooms. Brand was again sent aloft, while Barney Reilly and Bryson were detailed to work the bilge pumps. Peter Currie was told to scrub the deck of the crew's berth in the forecastle.

For the boys on the deck this cold was hard to bear. Within an hour neither John nor Jimmy had any feeling in their bare feet, which were blue. Jimmy's clothing, full of holes, could not have given much insulation against the strong wind and he was shivering, his teeth chattering uncontrollably.

Hughie, on the after deck house, had taken refuge from the wind between the two boats and was working on the other gunwale. Even so his hands were so cold and wet that he kept dropping the scraper and, more than once, had to retrieve it when it clattered to the deck below.

The sleet turned, through the day to snow, which began to settle on various parts of the ship, but not on the decks which were too frequently rinsed by the heavy sea.

As the light began to fade and the temperature dropped, icicles started to form on the roof edges of the deckhouses and snow settled on the poop and forecastle decks. The stowaways were still at work; Brand aloft in borrowed oilskins – he had been sent aloft to replace a sailor who had strained his back – the remainder engaged in menial tasks on deck.

During this time the ship was plunging and rising in a heavy sea which itself had a scum of melting snow. The deck was all the more slippery because of its steep angle of heel in the strong wind. The starboard side was high out of the water and snow was settling on the main and foredecks, while the waves rhythmically broke over the port gunwale, flushing the snow out through the freeing ports.

Neither John or Jimmy could ignore the pains in their bare feet. Their trousers had been sodden up to the knees, now they were frozen stiff.

Unable to bear it any longer, one by one the stowaways took shelter. John, Jimmy and Reilly were in the sail room when the Mate was seen coming out from his quarters.

"Quick, it's Kerr," said Reilly. They all grabbed brooms and sneaked on deck, scrubbing for all they were worth.

"Nice tae see ye busy," said Kerr, his words clouds in the brittle air. He stopped. "I can see Bryson; Brand's aloft; I know where Currie is; where's the Telegraph Boy?"

"I don't know where Hughie is, Sir," said Jimmy.

"Peacock?"

"I don't know either, Sir," said John. "He was round by the galley a while ago."

"You'd better not be givin' me the run around," said Kerr, as he walked off. The Mate's search of the area around the galley revealed no trace of the boy. Finally, he went to the fore hold and peered into its blackness. A small cough gave the boy away.

"Telegraph Boy!" shouted Kerr, his voice resonating in the hold. The boy came into the shaft of light and squinted timidly up.

"What d'ye think you're doin' down there?"

Hughie burst into tears.

"I'm.. so cold… my fingers are hurting so much… I can't… I can't…"

"You can and you will," interrupted the Mate. "Get up here now. Come on, move y'sel." Hughie climbed the ladder and, as he clambered over the hatch coaming, Kerr took him by the ear and marched him to the pin rail. Taking a rope's end he lashed the boy several times across the back and legs. "Now get back tae work!"

Released from the man's grip, Hughie ran off, crying loudly. He slipped on the icy deck and fell.

"Pick your feet up, you clumsy boy!" shouted Kerr.

John, shocked and angered by the beating and by Hughie's distress, surprised himself by shouting, "Leave him alone ye big bully!"

"Oh it's the Peacock calling," said Kerr. He walked towards John, who now bitterly regretted saying anything. The boy backed away as the Mate advanced on him.

"Come here, Peacock…" He beckoned. "Come on…"

John walked slowly up to the Mate. He knew what was coming and sought to stave it off. He put his hands up to shield his head.

"Don't you hurt me. I'll tell my Pa, then you'll be in trouble."

93

"Your Pa a good swimmer is he?" smiled Kerr, looking deliberately out to sea. Before John could find an answer, the Mate's gloved hand struck his head, knocking him off his feet. The man stood over him like a hawk over a cornered mouse. He smiled and kicked John in the stomach, winding him. He bent down and spoke quietly to him. "Little boys should learn when tae keep quiet." Leaving the lad doubled up, sobbing and groaning on the deck, he strutted off towards the stern of the ship.

Brand noted his approach and was seething inwardly at the violence meted out to the small boys. He avoided the Mate's gaze by looking out to sea. An unexpected slap round the face shocked him. Kerr put his face four inches away from his. The youth was standing against the wheel of the bilge pump and couldn't back off. The Mate spoke tersely.

"Work ye bastard, work! Ye can daydream when you're off watch."

The stench of whisky and tobacco was sour and strong on his vaporous breath.

## 12. *Bryson in trouble*

During the next few days, the weather remained very cold and blustery. The stowaways, in their inadequate clothing, were tortured by the cold and took every opportunity to take shelter, rather than work in the sub zero temperatures. This was noticed by Kerr, who himself appeared on deck only as much as he needed.

Depending on his mood and whether or not he had been drinking he either ignored their absence or sought them out and slapped, punched or kicked them, making them return to their duties.

The seamen were thickly clad, and over their warm clothes, oilskins were worn. The stowaways, thinly clothed, drenched by wind blown spray and occasional deluges of seawater, were neither dry nor warm. On one particularly cold day, their clothes froze stiff on them.

Bryson was on deck near the galley when Salton the cook came out and walked to the sail room (the biscuits were stored in a locker there.) As soon as his back was turned Bryson was in the galley looking for food. He came out seconds later with his pockets bulging, to find Currie standing there. Bryson tore him off a piece of bread.

"Not a word to anyone," he said sternly, as they trotted off to the forehold to eat their booty.

Several hours later Bryson heard his name being called and recognised the voice as Kerr's. He had been sheltering in the sail room, but took up his broom and pretended to be busy sweeping. He shouted back, "Here"

As the officer approached, Bryson could see from his expression that he was in trouble.

"You thieving layabout!" said the Mate, taking a length of rope from his pocket.

"What's the matter? What am I supposed to have done now?"

Kerr lashed him across the arm with the rope.

"I will not have stealing on this ship!"

"I've not stole nothin'," protested the youth.

"Ye were seen, ye liar. Ye were seen comin' outa the galley," spat Kerr, who then proceeded to give the youth further lashes. Bryson cowered from the blows, crying out in pain. "Get up on the forecastle head and stay there until I say ye can come down. I want ye where I can see ye. Move an inch an' I'll show ye how a real floggin's done." Bryson went towards the forecastle clutching his arm. A sudden call from the Mate stopped him. "Bryson, ye'll not need your coat. Drop it into the hold."

There was no bulwark on the forecastle head, only a railing, so there was no shelter from the clawing wind and penetrating spray. At stand down the stowaways made their way to the comparative warmth of the fore hold.

Brand, seeing Bryson leaning against the capstan, was puzzled.

"Where's your jacket?"

"In the hold," said Bryson, quaking. "Kerr made me take it off"

"Why?"

"Cause I took some food from the galley."

"It's stand down y'know."

"Aye, but not for me. I've tae stay here until he stands me down."

"Oh, d'ye want anythin?"

"Aye, my coat an' somethin' tae eat," said Bryson, "hot if ye can get it."

"I'll see what I can do," said Brand, climbing down the ladder to the hold.

"Christ, the stink gets worse every time I come down here. It smells of shit lately."

"I think someone's doin their business," said John.

"What, down here?"

"Aye," said John. "It smells awful strong over there." He pointed to a dark area of the hold. Brand walked across the coal to the area concerned.

"Johnnie, bring us the lamp." Reilly took the lamp and with John went over to look.

"Ugh, it smells vile! Look, there someone's tried tae cover it up wi' coal. Who the hell's doin' this? Christ, there's no excuse, the dunny's at the top o' the ladder."

"Kerr'll kill us if he finds it," said Reilly. "Christ, if the stink gets much worse it'll find him. Who did it?" He looked at the others.

"It wasn't me," said Reilly.

"Or me," said Hughie and John together.

"Nor me," said Currie, "I always use the dunny."

Brand looked at Jimmy, whose face was flushed.

"It was you wasn't it?"

"I thought we were allowed to. Jamie Bryson does it too; I thought it was alright."

"Bryson again! Well he can just bloody well clean it up and get rid of it or we'll all be for it. He might want tae live in a sewer, but I don't."

Brand turned to Jimmy. "Don't ye ever do your business down here again. Understand?"

"Aye."

"Ye better get a bucket and start cleanin' it up," said Reilly.

Brand turned to Reilly. "Bryson's in trouble anyway. He's been stealin' food from the galley."

"Aye, I know," said the Irishman. "He had a bit o' a whippin' I understand."

Brand nodded.

"Kerr's dolin' out a lot o' rough stuff lately."

"I wonder if the Captain knows how we're bein treated?"

"Dunno. Come tae think o'it, I've never seen him around when Kerr's dishin' it out."

"That's right. Perhaps we ought to speak to him about it."

"What we need is a deputation," said Brand.

"A what?" asked John.

"We all need tae go and see the Captain. Tell him we're bein beaten and starved. If we all go he might listen."

It was agreed that they would wait until Kerr was off watch and in his cabin then, when the Captain appeared on deck, they would approach him. Bryson was allowed into the hold at seven. Stiffly he climbed down, missed his footing and half fell on to the oakum. Jimmy was quick to try and help him up.

"Bugger off!" was the response as he pushed him away. This upset the boy, who thought he had found a friend. The youth staggered over to a corner of the hold away from everyone, pulled a piece of canvas around himself and laid down. He was still shivering with cold. Jimmy took his coat off, went over to Bryson and placed it across the youth's shoulders.

Brand decided to confront him about the fouling of the hold.

"Bryson," he said. There was no answer. The youth was rubbing some feeling back into his legs.

"Bryson," repeated Brand, a little louder.

The youth turned slowly to face him. His eyes were wet and red, his cheeks tracked with tears.

"What?" he said almost pitifully.

Brand's resolve softened.

"Nothin'. Are ye alright?"

Bryson nodded and turned away. Brand left him. Jimmy went over and sat beside him.

"What now?"

"I just thought I'd sit wi…"

"Oh, for Christ's sake leave me alone, can't ye?" He turned away from the boy and punched a bale of oakum. Jimmy got up and walked away. The others watched him. Reilly and Brand looked at one another; Reilly shrugged.

Jimmy felt a little lonely that night. He sat with the others and occasionally glanced in Bryson's direction. He opened his satchel and took out the letter. Although he couldn't read, his mother had read the letter to him so often that he knew it by heart.

His thoughts returned to home. The latest in a succession of 'new fathers' hated him. Several times his mother and this man had left him alone in the hovel that was home, to return in the small hours of the morning, drunk. Pretending to be asleep had not even been a defence, because the man had kicked him as he 'slept' on the floor, only to beat him further when he 'woke'. His mother, with glazed eyes, was too drunk to defend him from the brute. She never used to get drunk. Tears began to fall from his eyes. He put the letter to his lips and kissed it before replacing it in his satchel. It was then that he noticed that the little cloth bag was missing.

He gasped and began wildly searching the area in which he was sitting.

"Wha's up, Jimmy?" asked John.

"I canna find one o' me treasures."

"I'll gi' ye a hand – what is it?"

"It's a wee cloth bag wi' a couple o' bits in." They looked all around the area but found nothing. Jimmy folded and unfolded the letter and the drawing in the vain hope that it was in the folds. He began to cry.

"It could be anywhere."

Bryson smiled secretly, then putting on a serious expression, said, "See, I told ye you'd lose it." His hand went down to his jacket pocket, gently patting the bulge made by a tobacco pouch and pipe. 'Not a bad trade,' he thought.

Their chance to speak to the Captain came the following day. He was standing with the helmsman on the poop. The stowaways, led by Brand and Reilly, went up to him. Davie Brand was the spokesman.

"Captain Watt, may we speak to you please."

"In private," added Reilly, acknowledging the helmsman's presence.

The Captain looked puzzled.

"Why?"

Brand cast an eye on the helmsman before answering. Obligingly the Captain walked forward to the poop rail.

"We'd like tae see ye about the way we're bein' abused by Mr Kerr," said Brand. "All of us are bein' ill treated," he said, confidentially.

"Except Currie," added Bryson.

Somewhat surprised by the interruption, Brand ignored it and carried on.

"We are sent tae work in all weathers, ill clad as we are. We are beaten often, sometimes for no reason at all and we are not gettin' enough tae eat."

"And it's Mr Kerr's fault is it?"

"Yes!" they answered as one.

"He whipped Hughie with a rope," said John.

"Aye he did," said Hughie.

"I can't believe he'd do such things without good reason."

"I can assure you he did," said Brand.

"He enjoys doin' it," said Bryson, "Especially tae me."

"And you're not gettin enough tae eat?"

"No sir, the last three days we've only had one biscuit each," said Reilly.

"Mm…" said the Captain thoughtfully, "I hear what ye's sayin' and I'll see what Mr Kerr has tae say, seen from his view. I've always found him fair in his dealin's wi' stowaways, but I'll speak wi' him. Ye'd better get back tae work now."

"Thank ye Sir," said Brand, and this was echoed by all except Bryson, who just scowled as he walked away.

Later that day, Bryson and Brand were told to man the bilge pumps. As they turned the heavy iron wheels, Brand spoke.

"You've been doin' your business in the hold haven't ye?"

"What if I have?"

"Ye can bloody clear it up then."

"Why?"

"Cause it stinks. Ye'll have Kerr on our backs again."

"That'll make a change," sneered the youth.

"Look, I'm warnin' you – we're all agreed on this – you clear up your mess or we'll report ye tae Kerr. We're fed up wi' gettin in trouble 'cause of you."

"Oh, piss off," snarled Bryson.

Brand was furious and took out his temper by turning the heavy pump wheel with all his might. Gradually he calmed down. It was a while before he spoke again.

"Another thing – why did ye mention Peter Currie tae the Captain? We're all in this together."

"Oh yes?" came the cynical reply.

"Come on then, what do ye know that I don't?"

"He's Kerr's little spy."

"Rubbish."

"Look… he's the only one who knew I'd been in the galley. He was on deck when I came out. I gave him some bread, but he still told on me. That's why I got the whipping."

"I can't believe he'd do that."

"He spends a lot o' time wi' the crew, doesn't he? Never seems too hungry either."

"Don't forget, Bryson, he knew Kerr and the crew before we came on board the ship. He'd even run errands for Kerr's wife when we were in dock. I knew all this before we came on board. It was him who told me about the Arran."

"I still think he's a Judas, how otherwise would they have known it was me?"

Brand thought for a few moments. "Perhaps someone else saw ye."

"I looked around, there was nobody else watchin."

Brand was unsure.

"Ah well, I don't know then."

That evening, cold and damp, the stowaways descended into the hold. Unusually Bryson was the first down.

"Here comes the Judas," he said, as Currie descended.

"Leave him alone," said Brand.

"What's up?" asked Reilly.

"He reckon's that Peter's spyin' for Kerr – tellin' on us." He turned to Currie. "Are ye, Peter?"

"No!" said a surprised Currie, looking at the others and suddenly feeling vulnerable. "I know sometimes they treat me better than the rest of ye. My pa is a friend of Kerr's. Some of the crew are family friends too. I ran errands."

He looked from face to face and saw only mistrust or condemnation.

"I wouldn'a tell on ye!" he said in a trembling voice, "I hate Kerr as much as you do."

Bryson, a raking light falling on his stubbly, pock marked face, waved a grimy finger at the boy. "Well, I'm not taken in by that innocent look. He's a Judas alright."

"I'm not!" stressed Currie, bursting into tears.

"I'm not fooled by the waterworks either," said Bryson. "D'ye remember, Brand, when we hid in the hold? I'd stowed away wi' Jackie Hunter, an' when the cook came down he missed you an' me but found Jackie and Currie. Jackie was put ashore – why wasn't Currie?"

"I begged to be allowed tae stay on board," wailed Currie.

"On what conditions?"

"There weren't any conditions."

"Hah!" spat Bryson in disbelief.

"Bryson may be right for a change," said Reilly to Brand.

"I swear on the Holy Bible that I'm not a spy. I'm wi' you!" cried Currie emphatically, the tears washing clean tracks down his grubby cheeks.

"Cross your heart?" asked Hughie.

"Aye, cross my heart!" He crossed both hands dramatically over his chest.

"And hope tae die?" added John.

"Yes, and hope tae die."

## 13. *Snowballs*

Life on board the Arran was a daily struggle for the stowaways and their mood was gloomy, especially as each day the cold seemed more severe.

It was therefore with some degree of surprise that they were called on deck one morning to find that, not only was it light, but the sun was shining from a clear blue sky. More surprising than this, the decks were thickly quilted with gleaming snow.

"You've been up since four – if anyone asks," winked the sailor who roused them.

"Sure we have," said Reilly. " Workin' since four an' awake since foive. Where's Mr Kerr?"

"Off watch – Niven's on – He says ye can have some burgoo before ye start work. There's a lot o' snow tae get rid of."

The stowaways took their steaming bowls of porridge into the sail room to eat. They had strangely mixed feelings of privilege and guilt, about eating this unexpected meal. When the cook came into the room, everyone jumped and made efforts to hide their bowls.

" Good God, you're a twitchy lot! I've got some raisins for your porridge." He dropped a small handful into the offered bowls. "Don't expect this every day and, if ye value ye's lives, don't mention it to Mister Kerr."

Bryson pointedly gave a warning glare to Currie who, after catching his glance, looked away quickly and blushed.

After their porridge, the lads were given bread which they washed down with coffee. It was so long since they had eaten a proper meal that they found it hard to finish. The bread which remained uneaten they stuffed into their pockets.

Down in the stern quarters the Captain was working at his charts on the table in the saloon, the air richly fragrant with the smoke from his pipe. His mind, however was not on the ship's course but on the stowaway's deputation. Kerr knocked, entered the room and went to the w.c. in the far corner.

'Now's as good a time as any,' thought the Captain, and decided to speak to the Mate about the boys' complaints. Kerr came out of the toilet and closed the door.

"James" said the Captain. "A word."

"Aye?" replied Kerr brightly.

"Sit down a minute will ye?"

"What's this then, a bollocking?" he said, sitting down opposite Watt, who did not respond to the question.

"James ... the stowaways have complained that they're bein' badly treated. And, tae be fair, I've heard the same from some of the crew."

"So this is a bollocking is it. You'd rather believe the whining of a bunch of idle brats and a few soft seamen than me, would you?"

"I'm not sayin'..."

"Look, Sir..." The 'Sir' was spat more than said. "They're a shiftless, dirty and criminal bunch o' gutter brats. Bryson, their leader, has corrupted the smaller ones and they all look on you an' me wi' contempt."

Watt stiffened. Kerr noticed this and pushed his point home.

"They joke about us, take the piss, steal food and other things from the crew. Surely you wouldn't want me tae let that continue?"

Watt turned his mouth down at the corners and tapped his lip with his pipe.

"No, of course not."

The Mate continued.

"They have tae be disciplined, otherwise their nonsense will spread through the crew like a disease. Half the seamen are of an age with the older brats. You know how easily some o' them are led. I am teachin' them tae behave. It's beginnin' tae work. If I ease my grip now they'll fall back into their old ways."

"Ye say that they treat us wi' contempt?"

"Aye, they whisper and laugh at us behind our backs. There's no respect. They get the treatment they deserve."

"Alright James, I'm happy with that. We can't risk losing discipline."

Kerr stood up to go, then, on reflection, leaned across the table to put his face a few inches away from the Captain's. He spoke quietly.

"You know, I'm surprised that after all the time you've known me, you would believe that I would be less than just in my dealings with the stowaways. It doesn't sit at all well wi' me."

Watt felt both embarrassed and not a little intimidated by the Mate's tone.

"I'm sorry James. I had to ask. I didn't for a minute doubt you."

❖ ❖ ❖

Who threw the first snowball was unknown, but it struck Jimmy squarely in the nape of the neck. From then on there was a pitched battle between the stowaways. In the main, the snowballs were thrown in fun, but Bryson seemed to receive more than his fair share of missiles. These were not only of a firmer consistency but were delivered at a higher velocity than those received by the others. He seemed to take each missile personally and joined in the game with silent and grim determination.

The combatants peered round the deckhouses, sheltered behind the windlasses and masts in their cat and mouse games. The crew watched, laughed and began to throw the occasional missile as and when the opportunity presented itself. The stowaways returned fire.

Before long the deck became an arctic Trafalgar, port versus starboard, bow versus stern, with missiles coming and going in all directions. It was at this point, after hearing the sound of running on the deck above his head, that Captain Watt's growing curiosity forced him on to the deck.

A loose ball, unaimed, struck him on the chest. This seemed to Captain Watt to be a verification of the contempt in which Kerr said he was held.

"What the hell is going on!" he screamed.

The barrage waned and crew members hurried to resume their duties. The stowaways quickly took up their shovels and, with others in the crew, began to spade white clods of snow over the rail.

They worked steadily all day, supervised by the watch officers. By the evening the decks were largely clear of snow and were patchily drying. The Captain noticed Brand brushing snow from the main pin rail. He walked up to the youth.

"About your little deputation…"

"Aye Sir?"

"I have spoken tae Mr Kerr and I'm satisfied that he's treatin' ye fair. Ye's gettin the treatment ye deserve."

"But he's sendin us out tae work in this awful cold wi…"

"Look," said the Captain, pointing impatiently. "Look at those seamen. They have tae work in the cold. So can you. I told ye in the beginning, this is no free ride. Ye'll earn your keep."

"But…" Brand interrupted.

"Shut up!" Watt ordered. "I don't want tae hear about it. If ye've any complaints, direct them at Mr Kerr. As I said before, it's him who's dealin' wi' ye. I've more important things tae consider."

Before Brand could respond the Captain walked away.

Currie had been given the job of clearing the bilge pump area of snow and was concentrating on this when he became aware of a shadow blocking the lowering sun from him. He turned, squinting, to see the large silhouette of Bryson leaning casually on the main pin rail. The youth grabbed him by the lapels and pushed him backwards against the deckhouse.

"You say you're wi' us?"

"I am, I am," gasped a frightened Currie.

"Right then, prove it. Ask Kerr for some biscuits for us."

"Ask Kerr? He wouldn't… I couldn't… I… I…" He then burst into tears, being as much frightened by the Mate as by Bryson.

Bryson tightened his grip on the boy and banged him against the wall of the deckhouse.

"If ye don't, you'll have proved you're with them, and we'll have tae get rid of ye." He lifted the frightened boy off his feet to reinforce the threat. "It wouldn'ae take a second tae put ye overboard."

"I'll do it! I'll ask him. I will," squeaked Currie.

"Next time he comes this way I want ye tae ask him. I'll be watchin' ye … and listenin'. You tell anyone an' I'll kill ye, ye ken?"

The sighting a little later of Kerr, caused Currie to look round to see if Bryson was about. To the boy's dismay he was standing not many yards away and had also noted the Mate's presence on deck. Bryson signalled Currie to carry out his task.

The boy's mouth went dry as he slowly walked up to the dark bearded Mate. He spoke in a small, tremulous voice:

"Please Sir, can we have some biscuits, please Sir. We're awful starvin' Sir." Currie's chin trembled and his eyes filled with tears as he awaited the expected violent response. Somewhat surprised by the request, Kerr looked up from the boy, as if considering the matter and his eyes noticed a grinning Bryson peering around the corner of the deckhouse.

Pushing Currie aside, he approached the youth, who was too transfixed by this turn of events to run off. Without saying a word, Kerr punched Bryson on the nose. The youth fell backwards, cracked his head on the deckhouse and felt the warm sensation of blood coming from his nostrils.

Holding Bryson by the coat, Kerr turned to Currie, who was watching in confusion at what was happening.

"Did he make ye ask?"

Currie felt trapped; persecuted by everyone. Should he tell the truth and be put overboard by Bryson, or should he say it was his idea.

"I…" he stammered.

"I see…" said the Mate, kneeing Bryson hard in the groin. As the youth fell groaning to the deck, the Mate turned towards Currie, who was filled with horror at the sight of blood pouring from Bryson's nose. Fearing himself to be the next victim, in terror he wet himself and burst into tears. Kerr brushed past him and strode off, muttering.

## 14. *Hughie gets a beating*

Salton the cook returned from the sail room to the galley. He was walking with the steward and holding his cap on his head with one hand.

"Oh, I forgot to lock the biscuit locker" he said loudly, with a wink to John and Hughie, who were half-heartedly cleaning the brass fittings along the rail.

"I shall have tae go and lock it in a couple o' minutes" The boys looked at one another.

"You keep an eye out," whispered John to his friend, "while I go and get us a few biscuits."

"Oh no," said Hughie, "I'm not goin tae be the stoolie, you can do it."

"You don't have tae be a stoolie, just whistle if anyone comes."

"You whistle. I'll get the biscuits," said Hughie, as he made off to the sail room. John followed on to keep watch.

In the sail room Hughie reached up into the cupboard, taking out several biscuits and cramming them into his pockets. Outside, John had satisfied himself that no-one was about and stood by the mizzen pin rail, looking forward. A slight creak behind him made him turn around. To his horror the Captain was standing on the poop, having come from his quarters.

"Nothing tae do, Peacock?"

"Ah... Sir..." He thought quickly. "Up at the bows..." He then whistled as loudly as he dared.

"What?" said the captain quietly.

"There's something you should see... up at the bows, Sir."

He whistled again.

"What?" This time Watt's tone was more irritated. "Why do you keep whistling?"

"Er... I like whistling." He whistled again, this time more tunefully. "Whistling makes me cheerful; keeps me happy."

Watt did not appear convinced. John sidled around to the doors to the sail locker. He kicked the door with his heel as the Captain came down on to the main deck.

Seeing his friend outside, Hughie came out of the cabin.

"Got 'em," he said.

John winced as his friend spotted the officer.

"Got what?" asked the Captain. Hughie thought quickly.

"Er... a new cleanin' cloth." He pulled his cloth carefully from his bulging pocket. Unfortunately the biscuits had been put on top of the cloth and one came out with the rag, dropped onto the deck, rolled drunkenly towards the Captain's feet and, after describing two almost perfect circles, came to rest three inches away from the Officer's highly polished boot.

Before the boy could run he was grabbed by the arm.

"Turn out your pockets!" said Captain Watt angrily. Hughie took out the biscuits and shamefacedly offered them up to the Captain.

He shook Hughie roughly and with his other hand cuffed John round the head.

"Get out of my sight!" he said, as he strode forward, dragging the tearful boy behind him. John followed at a distance.

As he neared the galley the Captain shouted, "Salton!"

The cook came out. He looked surprised.

"What on earth are you doing leavin' food lockers unlocked. These festerin' brats'll steal anythin'!" He thrust the biscuits roughly into Salton's hands and continued, "Put them back in the locker, lock it and give me the key. I'll have Mr Kerr supervise the issue from now on."

He turned and, almost wrenching Hughie off his feet, dragged him to the fore pin rail, where he took up the end of a line and thrashed him a dozen times across the back and legs. Hughie writhed to avoid the blows and screamed as the rope hit home.

His anger spent, the Captain pushed the wailing boy against the deckhouse and prodded his chest with his finger.

"I will not have thieving on board this ship – that's just a taster of what you'll get if you're caught stealing again."

He marched off towards the stern of the ship.

Hughie, still sobbing, caught his breath and began a coughing fit. John came up, patted him on the back and put his arm round him. They sat down on the fore hatch while he recovered.

"Why didn't you whistle?" Hughie gasped between sobs.

"I did. I whistled as loud as I could but the Master was right by the sail room door."

"I didn't hear it. You're a rotten stoolie. Next time I'll be the stoolie and you can get the beatin'!"

As Kerr came from below the following day, he saw a small figure going under the forecastle head. Suspicious that the boy was dodging work, he crept up and called him out. It was Jimmy.

"Sir?" the boy enquired.

"What are ye doin' under there?"

"Nothin' Sir"

"Nothin'? Ye should be doin' somethin'. Have ye no task?"

"Aye, I've tae scrub the main deck." Kerr noticed a small yellow blob to one side of his mouth.

"You've bin' eatin under there, haven't ye? – Empty your pockets." He flushed and pulled out some buttered bread and a lump of beef.

"Beef. Did ye steal it?"

"No!" he said emphatically, "I didn't steal nothin'. I was give it."

"One of the other stowboys give it ye?"

"No Sir, I was give it official – by a sailor. He said he could spare it – said I looked hungry, an' I was Sir, I really was."

"Given by a sailor eh? Which one?"

"Can't remember, Sir." He began to cry.

Kerr took the beef and bread and threw it overboard. He gripped the boy's shoulder firmly. "You tell me if any o' the crew offer ye food, an' remember who they are. D'ye hear?"

"Aye Sir," he sniffed.

The Mate walked briskly off towards the stern quarters, descended and knocked on the Captain's door.

"Come in."

"Captain, the crew are feedin' the stowaways. We have tae stop it."

Captain Watt sighed.

"James, I'm sick o' these bloody brats. I wish we could get rid o' them, they're a sore on the backside."

"I know Sir. The crew are goin soft on 'em."

Watt tapped the table with his fingernails while he thought.

"Right! We'll ration the crew. Half rations. It's likely we're goin' tae have to anyway if we hit the ice, so we'll do it now, as a punishment for feedin' the brats. Muster 'em all on deck now, will ye James?"

The crew were mustered on the main deck and were addressed from the poop by the Captain:

"It seems ye have food tae give away tae the stowboys. I won't have them bein' fed grub they've not earnt. Ye'll be on half ration from today an' if I hear o'anyone givin' the brats food, I'll have him chained tae the forecastle head an' dock his pay. Understood?"

A dispirited "Aye Sir" rippled out from the company.

"Right. Dismissed."

"I knew them little sods'd drop us in it," said Jeremiah as he turned to go back to his task, "now we're sufferin' for it."

"I'd throw the bastards over the side – have done wi' it," said another.

As the day wore on the weather deteriorated. The sky was almost a metallic grey and the ship began to pass ice floes. At first these were small and isolated, but as the hours went by they became larger and more numerous, grating against the Arran's flanks or being crushed by the bow. It was sleeting hard and all the stowaways were wearing every stitch of clothing that they had, in an attempt to keep themselves insulated against the biting cold.

Hughie had tied the earflaps of his cap under his chin, but still his ears were purple and singing with pain. The others had tied their caps on with lengths of canvas, which also gave some protection to their ears. Even the seamen, well insulated against the cold, were finding the conditions hard to bear.

The sea became rougher and huge thunderclouds blackened the horizon. Before nightfall the stowaways were thankful to be ordered below into the comparative warmth of the hold. The hatch was battened down to await the storm but they were too cold to care.

The storm lasted all night and when, in the morning, the hatch was opened the boys greeted the light with mixed feelings. They could hear the wind whining through the rigging and sleet could be seen falling into the hold. By now they were reasonably warm, having huddled together all night. They hated the black stench of the hold, but it was heaven compared to the numbing cold that awaited them on deck.

Wrapped as warmly as possible the stowaways went on deck. The chill of the air made their nostrils sting. Hughie had a sneezing fit and before long they all felt the familiar aches from tensing their muscles against the extreme cold.

During the day they took every opportunity to shelter: sometimes in the hold and at other times in the forecastle. The sail room was a refuge to be used with care, as its doors were opposite those of the stern quarters, and officers were prone to appear without warning, as Hughie had found to his cost.

None of the stowaways had been fed since breakfast on the previous day and all were ravenous. At lunch time the smell of cooking from the galley was a kind of torture for the boys. Finally, Jimmy saw his chance when Salton took food down to the saloon for the officers, leaving the galley door open. After a quick look round he nipped into the galley, scooped up some breadcrumbs, funnelled them into his mouth, but was unable to find much more to eat.

In desperation he rummaged through the waste bin and found some meat and a soggy, mildewed biscuit that had more than its fair share of weevils. Wiping the insects away as best he could, he stuffed the fatty grey meat and the musty biscuit into his mouth and made a quick exit. Bryson later stole four biscuits from the forecastle and took some tobacco.

As the day passed the wind eased, the sleet stopped and patches of blue sky poked through the blanket of grey. Kerr ordered the hatches to be completely removed to ventilate the holds. The storm had displaced some of the cargo in the main hold. Some of the crew, with Brand, Reilly and Bryson, had been detailed to put the hold back into order. When this was complete the forehold was next to receive their attentions.

"Bloody stinks down here," said one of the seamen, as he descended the ladder. This hold was in better order generally than the main hold and was partially stocked with bales of oakum, the remainder being coal, with a few casks here and there.

"If we move a couple of these bales over," said a sailor, "they won't keep getting the coal fall between them. Gi' us a hand will ye Reilly?" The Irishman obliged and both men bent to lift the bale.

"Ugh, what's this?" said the seaman, dropping the bale and holding up his hand to inspect it.

"Christ, it's shit. Oh God, that's disgustin'!"

He wiped his hand on the oakum and called out to one of the other sailors working in the hold.

"Get Mister Kerr will ye. I think he should see this. The dirty bastards have been shittin' in the cargo. Christ, it stinks too! It's bloody evil."

After Kerr had seen the fouled cargo he ordered all the stowaways below and stood, fuming, at the foot of the ladder.

"Right then. Which of you brats has done this?"

Brand would have wished to blame Bryson, but didn't because, for all the problems he caused, it was still Kerr who was the enemy. The stowaways had to stick together. There was no answer, and all the stowaways accepted the subsequent beating in silence.

With Kerr standing over them, rope in hand, they were made to search the dirty bales of oakum and the coal, for faeces. Altogether five bales were soiled and the stowaways were made to pull the fouled rope yarn from the bales and throw it overboard.

This was an utterly distasteful task and several of the stowaways retched as they worked. When the task was completed to Kerr's satisfaction he called them together.

"Not only do ye steal from us, but ye destroy our cargo. Yet, ye expect us to feed ye and carry ye to the New World. For two pins I'd throw the lot o' ye over the side, but then we have tae go by the law -- more's the pity. Law or no law, any more foulin' o' the cargo an' ye's dead – the lot o' ye'. De ye hear me? Not beaten; not deprived of rations; ye's dead!"

A subdued 'Aye' reassured him that the message had been understood. Kerr moved to the foot of the ladder and turned to look back at the stowaways.

"Have ye any idea what kind o' diseases ye can get if ye do this kind o' thing. It would go through the ship like wildfire." He began to ascend and stopped a little way up the ladder. "Don't bother askin' for somethin' tae eat. When ye merit feedin' I'll see you're fed."

Bryson sat on a bale of oakum biting his nails and looking sheepish.

"I was a fool, sure to God," said Reilly. "Why didn't I let Kerr push him overboard. Now I've had a beatin', thanks to him and his filthy habits."

"Are ye proud o' y'sel now," said Brand, "little boys like Pauley, McGinnes and McEwan have been thrashed because o' you. Don't you ever do anythin' like that again."

Bryson casually nibbled his fingernails and pretended to ignore him.

## 15. A bad night

John found it particularly difficult to sleep that night. He had been chilled to the marrow all day and he was only just beginning to thaw out. To add to this, he kept getting pains in his stomach: no doubt caused by lack of food.

Gradually the spasms of pain decreased and exhaustion allowed him to sink into sleep's gentle cradle. Hughie was lying close to him, his breathing verging on snores. As John slipped into unconsciousness, his friend had a sudden coughing fit, which woke him again. It was not so much the sound, as the jerking of the boy's body that shook him into wakefulness. Hughie, by now used to having these coughing fits, did not wake up.

John lay on his back, listening to the sounds of the ship. How different was the reality, from the romantic vision that he had conjured up while traversing the imaginary seas and lands on the ceiling at home. In his nightly imaginations in Greenock he had been a hero, a bold adventurer achieving fame and fortune. This living nightmare could not be more different. He felt a stinging sensation in his eyes and nose and a tear ran from the outer corner of his eye, back and into his ear. Hughie moved again and grunted and he could hear someone else groaning.

His thoughts returned to Greenock.

'The primroses will be out in Well Park,' he sniffed, as he remembered how, on one Sunday, he had been chased by the 'parkie' when he had picked some to take home to his mother. She had put them on the dinner table. 'I wonder what it was we had? Was it pork, with tasty, chestnut-coloured, crunchy, crackling and crispy, glistening, golden brown roast potatoes, glorious, green cabbage and Maw's gravy ... wonderful, rich and dark brown... Cabbage? Why is my mouth watering at the thought of cabbage? I never even liked it. I could eat a ton of it now...' He deliberately broke that train of thought as it only seemed to make the pains return. His thoughts returned to Well Park...

'Maw was always glad to see the primroses. She used to say they were the way that spring told winter to go away, and the yellow was to remind the sun to come...'

His thoughts continued and he imagined lying on the grass in the park, running his fingers through its cool greenness, breathing in the sweetness of its newly-mown fragrance. 'The fruit trees will be in blossom soon...' His thoughts went back to the previous spring and the trees in Mr Campbell's garden. 'How heavy were the trees with the pink and white blossom, and how, when it fell, the petals drifted in the gentle breeze and looked like snow on the ground. How nice it would be to see these things instead of the endless, bleak grey swell of the ocean, with its salty stinging wind.'

He thought of the winter evenings at home... of sitting in the range's rosy glow, warming his toes by its heat, with the appetising smell of bread gently toasting on the end of a fork.

John was weeping now as the memories formed pictures in his mind. 'Rosie will be pork and bacon by now, with half her flank hung up the chimney to smoke. There'll be one, or maybe two, piglets in her place. Piglets are funny. I bet they'll soon be all grown up. Rosie didn't seem to be a piglet for more than a few weeks. She was a good pig. She was more than a pig, she was a friend; I could talk to her. I bet she made good bacon and wonderful sausages.'

His tearful reminiscences were suddenly interrupted by a gasping and gurgling sound from Hughie. The boy began to thrash about and, as John turned to face him, he sat bolt upright gasping for breath.

"What's up. Are you alright?" asked John.

Hughie breathed a sigh of relief. "That was horrible! I felt I was suffocatin'. It was really strange… Everythin' was alright, then suddenly I was freezin' and couldn't hear nothin' 'cept my heart beatin' and I couldn't breathe. Oh Johnnie it was awful. I felt I was dyin'."

The boy lay down and puffed in relief.

"Sounds 'orrible." said John. "I've been thinkin' about home…"

"An' I've been thinkin' about gettin' some sleep," interrupted Bryson, "It's like a three ring circus over there. D'ye mind shuttin' up?"

"Miserable bugger," whispered John to his friend.

Before long Hughie was snoring and John felt irritated that he was the only one who seemed to be awake. Try as he could, he was not able to sleep. He had tossed and turned, laid his head this way and that – all to no avail. He didn't exactly feel uncomfortable, but he couldn't ever remember feeling quite so conscious of his feet. They felt hot and fizzed like sherbet. Now and again it felt as if a tiny mouse, with scratchy claws, had run across their soles, making them jump involuntarily. After what seemed like hours of enduring this sensation, at last, he found himself drifting into the cotton wool cloud of sleep.

It felt as if he had only been asleep for a matter of minutes when a cry rang out, waking him.

"Oh God!"

"I'm sorry!" The voice was Jimmy's.

"Christ, what made ye do that?" said Currie.

"I thought it was just a fart," he said, "I'm awful sorry."

"It's all down my side – oh God, it stinks."

"I canna help it. Ive had the guts ache all night." He began to cry.

"What's up now?" Bryson was irritable.

"Jimmy McGinnes has shit himself an' it's all gone on me," said Currie.

"Bloody hell!" exclaimed Brand, his voice gruff from sleep, "that's all we need! Kerr'll go berserk if he finds out."

"Well, he better not find out then," said Reilly, "No reason why he has to know."

"Unless some little worm tells him," said Bryson, looking at Currie.

"I'm not a tell-tale and I won't tell about this!" He began to whimper. "It's not fair, I've never told." Brand began to help Currie out of his soiled clothes.

"Phew this smells evil! Bryson, get us a bucket o' water will ye?"

"Get it y'sel."

125

"I'll get it," said Reilly irritably.

"Should of thought that McGinnes would have grown out o' doin' that," moaned Bryson. "What is he, a big baby? Perhaps we should gi' him a nappie. Find him a wet nurse too. Bloody nuisance! All this in the middle o' the night…"

Reilly threw back the canvas of the hatch and climbed out on to the deck. The wind, still cold and strong, tore at his hair and made his eyes water. Sleet could be seen, falling in thin needles, against the dim light of the deck lamps. These gave just enough light for him to see what he was doing.

Using the seawater pump by the water closet he drew some water. The bucket was almost full when he heard a voice behind him.

"And what are you up to?" It was Niven, the Second Mate. "Not like you tae be up before ye's called" The sound of raised voices could be heard coming from the hold.

"What's goin' on down there?" He went towards the hold, peered into it and finally went down the ladder. Niven screwed up his face in distaste.

"What a stink. What's happened?"

Brand answered. "The lad's had a bowel upset, Sir. It's alright, we're clearing it up. He couldn't help it Sir."

"Get the boy on deck and all the clothes. I don't want any water brought into the hold."

Back on deck Niven called out to one of the seamen, "Harley, come here." He turned to Jimmy, shivering by the rail. "Get all your clothes off." The boy reluctantly obliged and stood with his arms wrapped around himself. "Wash him will ye

Harley. He's messed his drawers." He touched Reilly on the arm. "And you lad, can wash the clothes."

"I get all the nice jobs, don't I?" moaned Harley, as Niven walked off.

"Ye mean all the big jobs, don't ye?" joked Reilly. Harley was not amused.

Minutes later Jimmy was clean and was told to run naked around the deck, to dry and warm himself. John was ordered to run with him to keep him company.

Almost as the day dawned the sleet stopped, but the cold was as hard to bear as usual. Jimmy spent a fair amount of his time on the toilet and was finally allowed below, as it was clear that he was unwell.

During the morning one of the crew slipped on the deck and wrenched his back. His place was taken by both Brand and Reilly. They were, at least, given some breakfast and oilskins to wear.

Towards midday it began to snow and soon the deck houses were thickly quilted in white. The boys again sheltered as much as they could and were subjected to cuffs and kicks from the Mate whenever they were caught idling.

The twin ravages of the cold and the lack of food was telling on the stowaways. Hughie was incapable of working for more than a few minutes at a time. He frequently became giddy and his cough was getting worse. Often the coughing fits ended up with him retching and bringing up blood.

The young boys, apart from Currie, who was still receiving food on the quiet from both the mate and the crew, were listless. They felt desperately weak and tired and were often tearful. Even Bryson had been seen with red, wet eyes at times.

Bryson, John and Hughie were sweeping the snow from the decks under the watchful eye of Kerr, when they noticed one of the crew go on to the poop to talk to him. They could see the seaman point in their direction occasionally and knew that they were the topic of conversation.

"What now?" muttered Bryson as the Mate walked towards them.

Kerr knocked the deck brush from Bryson's hands and pushed him backwards. The youth staggered but stayed on his feet.

"Turn out your pockets," said the Mate, thrusting him back against the rail. Bryson fumbled in his pockets as if trying to empty them, while leaving something inside. Kerr noticed this and brushing Bryson's hand aside, reached into his pocket. He pulled out an oilskin pouch containing tobacco.

"Where d'ye get this?"

"I found it on the deck – thought someone had thrown it away."

"Liar!" said Kerr, giving Bryson a jab in the stomach which winded him. "Ye stole it from the crew's quarters didn't ye, this and some biscuits?"

"No I didn't. I told you, I found them."

Kerr pushed him sideways and he staggered. "Get round to the main pin rail."

Bryson was reluctant.

"Move!" said the Mate, again pushing him towards the mast.

When they reached the pin rail Kerr took hold of Bryson with one hand and, taking the tail end of a length of rope, struck him ten times. Bryson screamed with pain at every lash and when the beating was over he fell on his knees. Kerr grabbed his stubbly hair and pulled so that the youth's gaze was directed at him. "Go and get a capstan bar. I want you tae keep sentry on top o' the galley, where I can see ye."

Bryson returned with the capstan bar and climbed the ladder. Once on top he stood still, waiting.

"Slope the bar, like a soldier does a rifle."

Bryson looked blank.

"Put the bar over your shoulder," said Kerr, in as patronising a manner as he could manage. "Now I want you tae walk the length o' the house, turn round when ye reach the end and say 'All's well that ends well' and then walk back tae the other end and, again, say 'All's well that ends well'. You'll do it until you're relieved. I'll be listenin' out for ye." Bryson, the dirt on his face smeared by the tears he'd shed, put the heavy capstan bar over his shoulder.

"That's it…" said Kerr, with heavy sarcasm, "Now let's see if ye can march like a soldier."

Bryson began trudging through the snow on the roof.

"March, damn ye! – March smartly – like a soldier would!"

Bryson straightened his back and marched, sending snow flying as he did so.

"That's better," said the Mate, chuckling.

Bryson reached the end of the deckhouse and turned, mumbling the words he was told to recite.

"Can't hear ye – say it loud."

Bryson repeated it louder.

"Still not loud enough. I'm goin' up tae the poop. I want tae hear ye from there. Say it again."

"All's well that ends well!" shouted Bryson.

## 16. *Bryson finds a meal and regrets it*

John looked at the others when they had finally returned to the hold. All looked gaunt and exhausted. Talk, now, was unwelcome and, for a while, all they wanted to do was rest. Bryson was again filthy and unshaven. He was biting his nails and staring into the black recesses of the hold as if deep in thought. Brand eventually broke the silence:

"It's the fourth of May today."

There was a silence as the others waited for him to continue.

"Is that supposed to mean somethin' or have you slipped your moorin's?" asked Reilly.

"We've been almost a month at sea – we stowed away on the seventh of April."

"A month? Is that all? Seems like a year," replied the Irishman.

"We must be gettin' close now," said Brand, earnestly hoping that it was so.

"Lot o' ice about though – I'll believe we're there when we're tyin' up at the docks."

"Aye, one o' the crew said he did this run in sixty six at this time o' year an' they were stuck in the ice for a month or more."

"That's it, cheer me up," said Reilly.

Brand looked over to Bryson, who was grimacing.

"What's up Bryson, don't ye like the idea of another month in this tub?"

"It's not that. I got guts ache. Are they ever gonna feed us again? I've had nothin' for two days now."

"We haven't had much either," said Jimmy. "Just a biscuit yesterday. When I get off this ship I'm gonna stuff m'sel 'til I'm sick!"

"Me too!" said John.

"I'm thirsty," said Reilly. "Dry as a bone. Kerr's rationin' the drinkin' water now. He's locked the pump."

"He hasn't?" said Brand incredulously.

"He has. I asked him for a drink o' water earlier and he refused me – said we'll need every drop if we get fast in the ice. 'If you're that thirsty' he says, pointin' at the sea, 'there's plenty o' water out there. So I ate some snow – might as well be as cold inside as out. It tasted better than the stuff from the pump though."

Hughie gave a little cough, which caught in his throat and developed into another eye-watering coughing fit.

"For Christ's sake stop that bloody coughin!" said Bryson. "Cough, cough, cough, day and night, every day. I'm sick o' the sound o' it."

"D'you think I do it on purpose?" spluttered Hughie, his face red and his eyes wet.

"He can't help it, leave him alone," said Brand.

Bryson tuned sharply to face him.

"You gonna make me, heh? Come on then." He prodded his hand into Brand's shoulder. The youth turned his back on the aggressor, unwilling and too tired to be drawn into a fight.

"Oh, grow up, Bryson," he said.

"Don't you tell me tae grow up," he snapped and launched himself at Brand.

They punched and kicked at each other as they rolled from the oakum on to the coal.

Despite his humiliating beating by Kerr, where brain and experience had proved more important than size, Bryson was nevertheless as strong as a bear, and Brand knew he was getting the worst of it.

Reilly jumped on to Bryson and pulled him away.

"What's the matter with you? Don't youse think we've got enough trouble without fightin' one another?"

"He told me tae grow up."

"Ah, well, just let it go."

Currie, fearful that Bryson might turn on him, withdrew into the shadows of the hold.

Bryson angrily stamped across to the ladder, went on deck, beat his fists on the rail and screamed into the endless black void of the ocean. His vision was misted by brimming tears, torn from his eyes by the buffeting wind.

"Oh God, when will this end?" he muttered to himself. His tears began to flow freely and he seemed oblivious to the cold bluster of the wind and the stinging spray. "Oh Paw, why did ye have tae leave us?" he wailed, "Will I ever find ye?"

In the relative quiet of the hold Reilly was dabbing Brand's split lip with a grubby kerchief.

"Tis swellin up a treat," he said.

"Look at me, I'm filthy," said Brand brushing his trousers with his hands."

"Tis only coal dirt. It'll wash off."

"I just don't understand Bryson. I've tried talkin' tae him. You can't get through."

Reilly lowered his voice: "He did talk to me once, when we were scrapin' spars. He asked me not to tell anyone else, but I reckon he owes you an explanation. His father left home and went to America eighteen months ago – he's a tinker. Bryson was quite close to his Paw. He misses him and went off the rails a bit when he left. Got in with a bad crowd; started stealin – that's what he was gaoled for – stealin' brass."

❖ ❖ ❖

Bryson gradually became aware of the cold. He looked back along the deck and saw a pool of light by the galley. Edging quietly along he was surprised to find it unoccupied. He warmed his hands by the stove and looked for something to eat.

There was nothing edible in view and the cupboards were locked. He could smell food and traced it to the waste bin. Like Jimmy he rummaged through this and ate what he found: potato and turnip peelings, some fat and the remains of something unrecognisable, but jelly-like and slightly bitter tasting. There was some paper that had lard smeared on it. He first licked off the lard, then ate the paper. Thinking that he'd already been there too long, and fearing discovery, he left the galley and returned to the hold. He looked around: all the other stowaways were asleep and looked so peaceful.

How could they find sleep so easy when he found it so hard? He sat down on a bale of oakum, nibbled at his fingernails and stared, with swollen, wet eyes, at the flickering yellow flame of the lamp.

❖ ❖ ❖

When the sun began to rise as they worked on the following morning they were amazed to see the horizon completely white. What appeared to be solid ice was, in fact broken pans of ice of various shapes and sizes liberally sprinkled on the heaving sea. Many of these grated along the hull of the Arran as she ploughed through the water.

Jimmy felt particularly low. He still felt listless and weak and was still brooding about the loss of the ring and coin. He had looked all over for them, to no avail. Reluctantly he had come to the conclusion that Bryson had stolen them, as he was the only one who knew of what was in the satchel, but he had no proof.

Bryson was becoming more withdrawn and spent his spare time on his own and, although not hostile to Jimmy, he made it clear that he preferred his own company.

The chill of the wind was particularly hard for Jimmy to bear that day. His shirt, already torn on the side had gone through on both elbows in the past week. The jacket was hardly more than frayed rags. There was little defence against the cold. He scrubbed the deck, working the small headed broom along the line of the wet decking. He heard laughter and looked over to the main hatch where John and Hughie were sharing a joke.

His eyes filled with tears. Leaning his broom against the fore deck house he went into the sail room and threw himself, weeping, down on to one of the folded sails. He pressed his little satchel to his cheek and rocked gently. Opening it he took out the portrait. It was now so smudged as to be barely visibly, but those kind eyes, so full of good humour, still looked faintly out at him.

He could remember his father carrying him on his shoulders and showing him how to whittle wood. He always looked forward to his paw coming home from sea. They were happy days; the sun always seemed to be shining and although they weren't well off, he never seemed to go short of anything.

How life had changed. He now wore rags and when the soles of his boots had finally gone through there was no money left for repairs – it had all gone on gin and cheap whisky. He had made his escape from the latest, brutal, 'father' to a new life even more harsh and lonely.

With fingers stiffened by cold he took out the letter and ran his thumb over the writing. The ink was smudged in places where it had been wetted and the outer quarters of the paper were stained brown by the dye from the satchel's leather.

The door to the sailroom flew open.

"So there ye are," said Kerr. "What d'ye think ye's doin' in here?"

"Sir ... I was so cold, I..."

"D'ye think I'm feelin' warm? We're all cold. A bit o' work'll warm ye up. Wastin' ye's time readin' letters won't keep ye warm."

He pulled the boy to his feet, snatching the satchel and its former contents. Out on deck he held the 'treasures' in front of him.

"I won't have time wastin' "

"No!" shouted Jimmy, as Kerr threw the satchel and papers over the side.

❖ ❖ ❖

It had only been a matter of a few hours since Bryson had eaten from the bin, but he now felt sick and the pains in his stomach, rather than being relieved by his meal had, if anything, been increased. He asked Reilly to tell the deck officer that he was unwell and would not be able to work.

"I'll be the judge o' whether or not he's capable o' work. Get him on deck." said Niven.

Bryson felt weak and certainly looked pale beneath the layer of grime on his face. He found it quite a task just to climb the ladder, and when he made the deck he shuffled listlessly up to the second Mate.

"What's the matter then?" asked Niven.

"I feel rotten ... sick ... got guts ache."

"You'll live. Probably a bit o' a chill. Ye can wash the floor o' the crew's quarters; out o' the cold. That won't be too strenuous, will it?"

Bryson looked dismayed at the thought of work but felt too drained to argue. He had just filled a bucket of water from the seawater pump when he felt a cold, clammy numbness creeping over his face. He knew he was going to be sick and leaned over the gutter by the rail as the sickness spasms developed.

The effort in vomiting was such that he messed his trousers. As he moved, the warm slippery feeling slowly spreading downwards revolted him and he wondered what to do. He felt ashamed, particularly since his condemnation of Jimmy. Moving awkwardly to the ladder, after a quick look round to see if anyone was watching, he descended into the hold. He removed his trousers carefully. The smell was offensive and it was all he could do to avoid retching again. Wiping himself with the unsoiled parts of the trousers he changed into a pair that one of the crew had given him.

Climbing again to the deck, he hid the soiled trousers under the forecastle head, intending to wash them as soon as he had the privacy and the stomach to do so.

Towards midday snow began to fall in large flakes from a dull pewter sky. It blew in clouds like blossom in a windy orchard and spiralled in eddies around the sails. Bryson had finished below and was again working on the deck. He had been to the w.c. on a couple of occasions but was still suffering from stomach pains and the urge to relieve himself. While helping one of the crew to haul on a line of rope he again messed his trousers a little, but had no option other than to carry on working.

Shortly afterwards he saw, out of the corner of his eye, some activity up by the forecastle head. One of the seamen was pointing to something under the deck. Niven arrived and another seaman , with a boat hook, dragged the trousers on to the open deck. After a moment or two, Niven walked briskly off towards the stern quarters, a look of determination on his face.

## 17. Bryson takes a beating

Bryson knew that he was in trouble again and so hid behind the deckhouse, hoping to avoid anyone who was looking for him. He cautiously peered around the corner of the cabin, towards the stern. Apart from crew members going about their business there was little activity. He could hear his heart beating. 'Perhaps I'm jumping tae conclusions' he thought – 'why should they think it's me? It could be any of us – one of the crew even' But still an inescapable feeling of foreboding and shame crept over him. 'I'd better hide – no, why should I hide? I've done nothin' wrong. I'm not well. Even Kerr would understand that.' He pictured the Mate. 'No he wouldn't. He'd use it as an excuse tae gi' me another beatin'.' A feeling bordering on panic came over him. 'What can I do? 'I must hide. No. If I hide, sooner or later they'll find me – that'll only make the situation worse.'

He could smell his own excrement and knew that others could smell it too, but he had no other trousers and these were now soiled, so even if he cleaned himself up he would still smell. 'Perhaps Reilly could lend me some; I don't think Brand would help.' He thumped the deckhouse with his fist. 'Why didn't I think about this before. Now there's no time and I'm almost certainly in trouble.'

As he peered for a third time around the edge of the deckhouse he jumped with surprise as two strong pairs of hands grabbed his arms from behind.

"Mister Kerr sent us tae get ye," said the larger of the two men, "Good God, ye stink like a polecat."

Bryson struggled to get free. "Leave me alone. I'm not well: I've got a bowel complaint. Let me go." He managed to struggle free of the smaller man's grip and then tore himself from the grasp of the other. Turning the corner of the deckhouse as he ran away, he was stopped in his tracks by the sight of Kerr walking purposefully towards him, carrying the lead line.

The seamen again grasped the youth's arms and held him firmly. Bryson froze. There could only be one reason for Kerr to carry the lead line.

"Please Sir, I'm not well..." he pleaded. "I asked tae be let alone in the hold but they made me work. I..."

"Shut up," the Mate ordered. "Drop your trousers."

"No Sir, I don't want to."

"Oh, you don't want to, eh?"

"No Sir."

"Hunter, pull his drawers down," ordered Kerr tersely.

Hunter hesitated. "He stinks – he's shit himself."

"Just do as ye's told, will ye," said the Mate.

As his trousers were pulled down, Bryson began to whimper again. "It's no my fault Sir. I'm unwell – I really am. I tried tae tell Mister Niven but he wouldnae listen."

Kerr peeled off some of the line in a calm methodical way, as if measuring the optimum length needed for his coming task.

"You know what you are, Bryson?" he said, his eyes becoming wild and a tremor in his voice indicating that he was barely in control.

"I'm not well, I'm sick!" pleaded the youth.

"Aye, and I'm sick," said Kerr, suddenly lashing the youth's shoulder with the line, "Sick o' you. Take your clothes off."

"I'm really not well at all Sir, it's not my fault," he complained, his voice trembling as he began to undress.

He had stripped down to his vest when over Kerr's shoulder he saw the Captain approaching. He was aware that many of the crew and the other stowaways were gathering to see what was about to happen.

"Whew!" said Captain Watt as he approached, "I can smell the bugger from here."

"I'm not well," Bryson blurted out, his voice desperate, "I'm sick – I canna help it."

"I think ye's a filthy brat that needs teachin' a lesson. I think we've all had just about enough o' yer nonsense. Let him have it Mister Kerr."

Kerr needed no further encouragement, but grabbed the youth's arm and pulled him away from the seamen holding him.

"No, No, Please no!" Bryson pleaded, but his appeals fell on deaf ears. The first lash landed across his buttocks and the searing pain made the youth cry out. He writhed in an attempt to avoid the following blow, but it struck home across his hip , the rope end snaking round and lashing against his penis. He immediately dropped to the deck, his right knee gashing open on a deck ring. Bryson was gasping and while he was on his knees Kerr used all his force to beat the youth's back with the line. Three lashes in quick succession induced screams. The youth tried to stand and run away, but was again grasped by Kerr, whose grip on the lad's arm was so firm that his fingernails drew blood.

Bryson could no longer feel the individual blows. It felt like his back was on fire. The pain was unbearable and there was no let up in Kerr's fury. His lips were peeled back revealing glistening, stained teeth. The forest of his black beard was spattered with frothy spittle and his eyes were wild.

Bryson could hear, in a kind of detached way, his own voice screaming, yet somehow his mind was rising above the pain, which was so great that its surges were almost exquisite. It was as if he was in a dream. Perhaps he would soon wake up. Beyond his own screams he heard the voices of others and opened his clenched eyes to see the wavering, distorted forms of his fellow stowaways.

"That's enough – he's had enough!" shouted Brand, as lash after lash gave Bryson's torso the appearance of a well used cart track. Weals of red, blue and white appeared all over his body. Kerr pulled his victim's vest up to his shoulders and gave him further lashes. The vest had not given much protection against the blows, as could be seen from the marks already there.

Sinking on to his knees, Bryson gave up the fight and he hardly flinched as Kerr continued his frenzied attack. The other stowaways gasped.

"It's murder!" whimpered a horrified Jimmy.

"You're killing him!" wailed John.

"Enough, please stop – he's had enough – please!" shouted Reilly.

Currie and Hughie were crying and screaming "Stop!" at the tops of their voices.

More than thirty lashes were given before Kerr, panting, stopped his assault. Almost all the crew, both on duty and off, had witnessed the punishment. They were clearly shaken by the ferocity of the attack and murmured among themselves.

Bryson remained on his knees, seemingly unaware that the beating had ended. The Mate threw the rope down and wiped his mouth with the back of his hand.

Reilly and Brand moved forward to attend to the victim, but were stopped by the Captain, who barred their approach with a deck broom.

"Wait a minute," he said, "He's not finished with yet. He's still filthy an' needs a clean. Get up Bryson." The youth was doubled up and was softly moaning. Either he didn't hear the Captain's order or was incapable, for the moment, of responding. Captain Watt turned the broom and, holding the head, struck Bryson round the ear with the handle.

"Get up, damn you!" Bryson struggled to his feet.

"Take your semmet off" Bryson removed his vest, his face a mask of pain. He was visibly shaking from both shock and cold. In his nakedness the path of every lash was documented with a tartan of weals. The youth's face was pale and his eyes were glazed.

"Lie down." said the Captain.

Bryson only vaguely heard the command.

"What?"

"Lie down on the deck" He turned to one of the seamen. "Hunter, get some water from over the side. We'll scrub the brat clean."

Bryson lay down on his side, propping himself up on his elbow. He looked up blankly at the Mate.

"Turn on to your belly," said Kerr. Bryson complied submissively.

The Captain handed the broom to a surprised Brand.

"You'll need that in a minute," he said.

Brand looked at the broom. It was of a type used for scrubbing the decks. The head was fairly small with shortish, stiff bristles. He ran his thumb across them. They felt quite sharp.

The first bucket of water was dashed over the prostrate youth. He jerked and gasped at the impact of the freezing seawater and felt its salt sting where his skin was broken.

"Right, get to it Brand – scrub him," said Captain Watt.

Brand hesitated and at first began to gently brush Bryson's weal covered back. Despite Brand's attempts to be gentle the victim cried out with the pain. Brand lifted the head of the brush so that it barely skimmed the lad's skin.

"Are ye a great fairy, Brand?" shouted Kerr, "put some bloody energy into it will ye. Scrub the dirty bugger's arse."

Brand was unhappy with the situation, but had no option but to comply. The stiff bristles soon made his buttocks red and there were as many weals here as on his back. Brand could feel each of the raised ridges through the handle of the broom.

Bucket after bucket of water was dashed over the youth who cried out loudly and wriggled. The stowaways and others of the crew laughed at the youth's protestations because they believed that the broom was tickling him.

Bryson tried to get up, but Kerr stood over him, the lead line in his hand. "You try tae get up laddie, an' ye'll go down agin' a lot quicker! Now turn over." Bryson turned onto his back and winced as the weals pressed into the salt water on the deck. He drew his knees up and placed his hands over his genitals.

"Put your bloody legs down," said Kerr, kicking them, "and put ye's arms down by your sides. How can he scrub ye wi' them in the way?" Brand looked at Kerr, reluctant to start another bout of scrubbing.

"Go on!" said the Mate, "scrub his belly an' don't forget his weddin' tackle – we'll get the bugger clean if it kills him." This comment brought more laughter from the audience. Brand again tried to be gentle, but there really was no way that he could use the brush without hurting the youth.

As the brush was drawn across Bryson's penis and testicles, the victim drew his legs up sharply and rolled over on to his side. Brand then gently worked the brush over the youth's hip and outer thigh, hoping that this would satisfy Kerr.

Suddenly the broom was snatched from his hands by the Mate.

"Give it tae me, I'll show ye how tae do it!"

He pushed Bryson over on to his face with his foot and began to scrub the lad in earnest. The brush was driven hard, from knees to shoulders and back, pushing the struggling youth firmly into the deck. His shouts increased, much to the merriment of the audience.

John, as an onlooker was enjoying the event. He didn't like Bryson, or his dirty habits, and he did need cleaning. He took no pleasure in the beating but had watched with horrified fascination as lash followed lash. This was different, this wasn't a punishment it was just a cleaning and Bryson was finding it just too ticklish.

John wiped a tear of laughter away from his eye and looked over to Brand, who had withdrawn away from the area of punishment. Why wasn't he laughing too? He looked serious and actually turned away as the brush was worked between the youth's buttocks. John looked again at Bryson's face and realised that he was, in fact, in great pain.

The brush was driven up his back to his shoulder. This made Bryson draw his leg up, his damaged knee describing a red arc on the deck.

Little by little the truth dawned on the stowaways and some of the crew, and the laughter died away, to be replaced by a tense silence. Bryson's ordeal continued unabated. A further dousing of water was followed by even harder scrubbing. Bryson's skin was now a fiery red and little bits of skin began to peel off here and there. The seawater foamed and was becoming pink as little sparks of blood were brushed away.

The stowaways began to shout for Kerr to stop, but this was ignored. He worked the broom as if possessed. He was muttering oaths and kicking at Bryson as he writhed on the deck, and his red lips were wet with foamed spittle.

The Captain stood by, apparently impassively, watching the continuing ordeal. The only clue to his state of mind was that his hands were clenched and white knuckled.

After what seemed to be a lifetime, Kerr threw the broom down on to the deck and stood back.

"Get up!" he ordered, his voice husky. Bryson struggled to his feet, white faced and shaking. He looked unsteady, as if about to faint. The Captain handed him a bucket.

"Wash your clothes." he ordered.

The youth was beyond any disobedience and merely nodded. The Mate wiped his mouth on his sleeve and stood back.

The crew dispersed and the stowaways came forward to help Bryson.

"Clear off, the lot o' ye," said the Captain. "Leave him be."

John looked at Bryson. Little rivulets of blood were running down his body and one leg was red from the knee down. The crimson marks on the deck beneath his feet described only too clearly the agony of his ordeal.

## 18. *The Captains meet*

Bryson, naked, pale and shaking, put on his grubby vest. The effort of doing this hurt a great deal, the discoloured weals having now swollen to mimic the rope that made them.

Mentally, he felt strangely detached from his body and found it difficult to contemplate washing his clothes. There was no water in the bucket – the clothes weren't in the bucket either – how could he wash them?

The Steward appeared with a bucket of steaming water.

"Use this, it'll get the clothes cleaner," he said, offering the youth a cake of amber-coloured soap.

Bryson, still watched by the Captain and Mate, with trembling hands, fumbled the soiled clothes into the bucket and clumsily tried to raise a lather. He expected, from the amount of steam that the water was producing, that the water would be scalding hot, but was surprised to find it to be of a bearable temperature. This seemed to soothe his cold hands.

"I'll leave him with you," said the Captain, turning and heading for his quarters. Kerr nodded and lit up his pipe.

"When you've washed something, hold it up. I want tae look at it," he said calmly.

Bryson, beginning to focus on his task, without speaking held up a pair of trousers by the waistband.

"Let me look inside them," said Kerr.

The youth opened them compliantly. A brief glance satisfied Kerr that they were clean enough.

"Right, clean the other things like that, then wait here. I'll be back in a while." He shuddered in the cold, turned and went below.

It was half an hour before Kerr returned to find the washing done and spread out on the deck.

"Rig y'sel a line and hang 'em tae dry. Ye can sit on the galley roof 'til morning".

Bryson began to cry. He was already quaking with cold, his thin vest offering little protection. The punishment seemed never ending. Kerr noticed his renewed distress.

"Ye'll be warm by the galley chimney," he said, walking off.

Up on the roof, Bryson brushed an area clear of snow with his hands and sat as close as he could to the chimney. The sulphurous fumes and smoke stung his already swollen eyes, and while the radiated heat from the chimney occasionally warmed the nearest parts of his body, the gusts of wind blowing across the ship robbed him of any real benefit.

When the Mate had been below for a while, the cook came out from the galley and spoke to him.

"Come down for a minute. I've got some tea for ye." Without a word, Bryson descended stiffly to the deck and cupped his numb hands around the offered mug of steaming tea. He thought it strange that he couldn't feel its heat, but as sensation returned to his fingers threads of pain ran along their length; pain that finally subsided into a fizzing sensation.

"I don't think I can take much more o' this," he said, his eyes filling with tears. The Cook put his hand on his shoulder.

"Just try tae keep out o' trouble. Ye' seem tae be givin' the Master an' Mr Kerr the ammunition they need." He cut a large slice of crumbly bread and hacked a piece of cheese from the wedge.

"Here, take this, but keep quiet. I'll gi' ye somethin' hot tonight if I can."

Bryson had just begun to eat the bread when they heard someone approaching. He quickly stuffed the bread and cheese back into the Cook's hands. As if the food had been red hot, the cook quickly dropped it on to the worktop and threw a towel over it. A figure appeared in the galley doorway. It was Brand.

"Wha's up wi you two, ye look hellish guilty?"

"Oh, it's you," said Bryson, "We thought it was Kerr."

"I've brought ye your top coat," said Brand. As Bryson put it on and fumbled with the buttons he continued. "Look, we're all awful sorry for what happened. I was made tae scrub ye. Ye know that, don't ye? If it's any consolation I thought ye were very brave tae have taken what ye did."

Bryson turned his back and began to cry again. Brand, feeling awkward, made his excuses and left.

When he had finished his food, Bryson climbed up to the galley roof and made himself as comfortable as he could for the long, cold wait until morning. He idly watched his clothes flapping slackly in the wind and noted how often they were soaked by gusts of wind-borne spray. Water dripped from the trouser hems on to the deck and he knew that, placed where they were, they would never dry, but he was just too exhausted to move them.

The hours passed slowly. His mind went over all that had happened. How he now wished that it had been him rather than Jackie Hunter who had been found on board in Victoria Harbour and put ashore. Tears pricked his eyes.

'If only my Pa hadn't gone tae America. All these stories of fortunes tae be made turned his head... an' not a word from him since he left. He could be anywhere. He could be dead. Is there any point in tryin' tae find him? It's like lookin' for a needle in a haystack. I'm wastin' my time... The crew reckon we're goin' into the ice. It could be well into June before we get tae Quebec... How can I put up with another month of this? What else has Kerr got in store for me?'

A crack in the cloud allowed a shaft of silver sunlight to spangle the waves as they passed. The effect was almost mesmeric and, in different circumstances would have been quite beautiful. The rolling forms of the sea seemed to Bryson to be beckoning him.

'Perhaps that's the answer to it all... It would be so easy... There's nothin' for me in Greenock... there's probably nothin' but disappointment waitin' for me in America... There's no point at all in goin on... It would be easy... Just wait for night an' go up to the stern. In this cold it'd be over quick. No-one would see, they wouldn't even hear the splash.' He wiped a tear away from his cheek. Another few hours, that's all.'

As the long day began to draw to a close Bryson's cold numbed reverie was broken by a call from aloft. He looked up and saw a seaman on the foretop pointing out to sea. The line of the horizon was broken by the sails of another ship. She was schooner rigged and was a good way off but appeared on a similar, but slightly converging course to the Arran. When the last glimmer of light left the horizon she was still closing.

Salton, the cook, was as good as his word and gave Bryson some hot soup and afterwards some coffee. The youth ate silently and without enthusiasm. He felt hungry, yet full, and in the end it didn't matter. Salton closed his galley and spoke quietly to him.

"Look, the sail locker's open. Why don't ye come down an' spend the night in there. I'll be up before daybreak. I'll get ye up before Kerr comes on deck." Bryson looked disinterested.

"I promise," said the Cook.

Bryson clambered to the deck and headed towards the stern of the ship. He paused at the sail room and tried the door. It was, as Salton had said, unlocked. He closed it again and softly climbed the steps to the poop. He felt curiously calm, almost happy. Beyond the Arran's stern was total blackness, the only light being from the deck lights and the glow from the lantern light of the saloon below.

He had thought himself totally alone, but a movement by the stern stopped him in his tracks.

'Oh, God. I forgot the helmsman. How can I do it now, with him there.' Bryson felt irritated by the man's presence. The helmsman waved in recognition of his approach. Bryson did not respond. A sudden guffaw of laughter from the cabin below enraged him.

"The bastards!" The red heat of anger replaced the blue chill of resignation and he strode, muttering oaths and impossible threats, back to the sail room.

As the light climbed above the horizon it was seen that the schooner had outpaced the Arran and was now about a mile away and at anchor, her sails clewed up. She appeared to be fishing among the ice floes.

"A Frenchie," said Captain Watt, looking through his telescope,

"I think we'll pay her a visit; do a bit o' trade. A drop o' brandy perhaps."

The Arran backed her sails and stopped, as she approached within fifty yards of the schooner. The boat was hitched to the derrick, the wedges removed and the slack taken up on the lines.

The boat grated sideways along the skid beams, was swung out and lowered down to the sea. It fouled on a pan of ice and so was hoisted clear again while the ice was pushed away with a spar.

Three seamen climbed down the ladder to the bobbing boat, followed by Kerr, warmly wrapped in dark greatcoat and cap.

On the Arran the crew watched the small boat as it was manoeuvred between the ice floes. It was not as much rowed as fended off the pans of ice, which against the boat looked quite large.

John and Hughie were mechanically holystoning the poop as they watched the boat's progress. John thought that Kerr, who was sitting in the middle of the boat, had an almost regal air about him. He remembered hearing at school of Henry the Eighth being rowed along the Thames to Hampton Court. He would probably have had the same bearing, and the same degree of menace. 'At least he looks sober this morning.' he thought.

"I wonder what he wants wi' the Frenchie?" said Hughie.

"Wants tae do a bit o' trade I 'spect"

They watched as the Mate climbed aboard the schooner and shook hands with the French Captain. There seemed to be much arm waving and joviality as the two men talked. The raised tone of their voices could now and then be heard over the lap of the sea on the hull and the flapping of the sails as the crew trimmed them to hold the Arran still in the water. What the two men were saying could not be made out.

"I wish we were on that ship instead o' the Arran," Hughie murmured.

"What, wi' a lot o' foreigners?" said John, "Foreigners eat people y' know, 'specially fuzzy-wuzzies – they eat vicars as well."

Hughie nodded towards the schooner. "They aren't fuzzy-wuzzies are they?"

"No, fuzzy-wuzzies are dark brown. They're just Frenchies – they eat frogs an' snails an' dogs an' cats an'…"

"Ugh!" said Hughie, sticking his tongue out, "What about snakes, do they eat snakes?"

"Aye, an rats too. They eat anythin' that moves – 'cept people. Only fuzzy wuzzies do that."

"There aren't any fuzzy wuzzies in Quebec, are there?"

"Dunno, never bin there." John thought for a moment. "If there are, it'd be best tae take a pistol or a stick. Perhaps if you've got a stick they won't try tae get ye. Ye could gi' em a clout tae keep 'em off."

"What if they've got a stick too?"

"Run like buggery!" said John, dissolving into gales of laughter.

Their visit finished, the small boat wove its way back to the Arran. Brand was working by the rail as the Mate came back on board. He was met by Captain Watt.

"A word, Sir," He spread an arm and ushered the Captain away from the youth, giving him a kind of triumphal glance.

"Well, how did ye get on?" said the Captain.

"I had an awful job tae understand what he was sayin', but I think he'll take two o' the brats. I said that we'd gi'em some meat an' biscuit tae sweeten the deal."

"Sounds fair enough. Shame he'll only take two, the older ones are gettin' too chummy wi' the crew again. We'll take all three over… y'never know."

The Captain returned and spoke authoritatively. "Brand, get Bryson and Reilly. All o' ye, get what ye own together, and be back here in five minutes, no longer. Understand?" He noted Brand's quizzical look and added, "You're goin' for a boat ride."

The Captain then turned to his Mate. "Mister Kerr, get Salton or McLean tae dig out… what shall we say…" He looked to the sky for inspiration, "a half hundredweight o' biscuit an' four pieces each o' pork and beef? Yes, that should gi'em a good incentive."

"What for?" Bryson asked when told what to do by Brand.

"I should think its pretty obvious. We've been told tae get our stuff together. He's probably gettin' rid o' us on the Frenchie."

"Can't be worse than this."

"Better the devil y'know," said Reilly.

Bryson tied his clothes into a bundle. "I'll be glad tae go. The sooner the better. No-one could be worse than Kerr."

Carrying their small bundles of possessions, the three were met by the Mate. "Come on, it was five minutes, not fifteen."

They watched as the food was lowered down and first Bryson, then Reilly and Brand and finally the Captain, climbed down to the jolly boat.

The little boat bumped and ground its way between the floes to the French ship. She was smaller than the Arran and a good deal more scruffy.

Captain Watt climbed to the deck of the schooner followed closely by the three stowaways and one of the seamen. The short, stocky French Captain looked Reilly, Bryson and Brand up and down in a rather puzzled way.

"The men you want," said Captain Watt, loudly and slowly, as if talking to a slightly deaf child.

"Quoi? Ah yes ze men," he turned to a passing sailor. "Ou sont Canot et Dubois? Amenez les ici – vite." The sailor scurried off.

"Un moment, Capitaine," smiled the Frenchman.

The two Captains looked at each other, each grinning inanely and trying to find something to say. Finally Watt spoke.

"They are hard workers."

The Frenchman appeared confused at first, but then the smile returned.

"Oui, yes, zey work good. Very good."

Two seamen came up to the Capitaine. One was tall, thin and stooping, while the other was even shorter and fatter than his Captain, with a large boil on his neck.

"Voila, ze men," he said, with the air of a magician producing a rabbit from a hat. Captain Watt's mouth dropped open slightly as he looked at the sailors.

"Pardon?"

"Your friend ask for two men. These I give you."

"No, I think you have got it wrong."

"Quoi? I don't understand."

Watt spoke even more slowly and emphatically.

"These men," he waved an expansive arm at the three stowaways. "I..." he pointed his hands to his chest "give them..." he waved at the three, "to *you*." He offered his arms forward.

"To *me?*" said the Capitaine with equally loud voice and emphatic arm waving, his eyes as large as the buttons on his coat. "Non, c'est impossible!"

"I will give you some meat."

The Frenchman looked blankly at him.

"Pork and beef and some biscuit. You can put the lads off at the next port, or where you like. It will be alright, anywhere in the world will do."

"Er..." The Frenchman smiled awkwardly, then raised his hands as if pushing something away.

"No, I think your friend is not understand. Is a mistake. I'm sorry. My English no very good." Brand and Reilly smiled at one another. Bryson looked disappointed.

The little group clambered back down to the boat. The Capitaine talked to the little group of matelots who had gathered at the rail to watch the Scots' departure.

"Est ce qu'ils pensaient vraiment que nous voulions leurs rejets?"

Captain Watt was mumbling similar thoughts and looked very sour, sensitive to the unintelligible, but obviously derisory, chatter and grins of the French.

"Come on, hurry up!" he said as Brand, the last one, tried to board the bobbing boat. As the seamen fended off from the schooner and began to pull towards the Arran, Brand looked at their ship. She was grazed about the waterline where the ice had grated, but otherwise looked clean and tidy and none the worse for her eventful voyage.

Bryson who, thirty minutes ago was excited and hopeful of escape from the Arran, returned with a heavy heart to what he now pictured as a large black coffin.

## 19. *Currie finds a thief*

William Salton the Cook had tried, whenever he could, to supplement the stowaways' meagre rations. Kerr however, still held the keys to the store lockers and daily supervised the issue of food.

They were fed according to his moods. If he was sober and in a good mood, they stood a chance of getting something to eat, but if he was drunk or in poor humour, they went without. It was then that the Cook did his best to give them food 'on the quiet.'

During one very cold, foodless day, Salton had given John, Hughie and Peter Currie some biscuit and salt beef on the condition that it would be eaten out of sight below.

Kerr kept the boys busy on deck but their empty stomachs and the unusual weight in their pockets nagged them to go below at the soonest opportunity. When the Mate went to his quarters the boys needed no further encouragement.

Moving into the hold they began their meagre meal. They had hardly begun when they heard the sound of movement on the half deck above their heads. The boys drew into the shadows.

"There isn't one open," said a voice.

"Then we'll bloody well open one," said another. Hughie's foot noisily slipped on the coal as he moved into a more comfortable stance.

"Ssh... what was that?" said the first man.

"What?"

"I thought I heard somethin'."

The head of a sailor appeared over the edge of the half deck. The boys silently drew further back into the shadows. Only Currie could see the seaman clearly, his face top lit from the open hatch above.

"You're imaginin' things. Gi'us your knife will ye?"

The boys continued to listen, trying to picture, from the noises, what the men were doing. They heard first the splintering of wood, then the grating of the cask on the decking.

"Open the bag wider damn ye! I'm spillin' more than I'm gettin' in. It's goin all over the place."

"I'm holdin' it as still as I can. I only got one pair o' hands. If we leave a mess here Kerr'll find it – Then there'll be trouble."

"Nah. If he kicks up we'll say it's the brats. Kerr'll be happy tae believe that." The other sailor chuckled.

"Yeah, say it's Bryson." They both laughed.

Two minutes later, the sounds of feet climbing the ladder to the deck echoed through the hold.

After a few moments Hughie whispered, "D'you think they've gone."

"I think so," replied Currie, peering cautiously out of the shadows.

They crept up the ladder to the half deck and found a cask of meal that had obviously been broached. Crude attempts had been made to reinstate the lid, but the wood was too splintered for this to have been effective.

"Let's get outa' here," said John, "before someone blames us."

John looked at Hughie and Currie and at the small mounds of meal around the kegs.

"A mouthful or two would do nae harm – it's spilt anyway" Neither of his friends needed further encouragement. They ate the dry meal as fast as they could. As it was so dry it was difficult to eat much. Hughie got hiccoughs and fought to control them.

Currie was first up the ladder and as his head appeared above the hatch coaming he saw Kerr further down the deck. Unfortunately, Kerr had been looking in that general direction when the boy's head appeared. As a reflex action he ducked down again.

"What's up?" asked John.

"Kerr's just outside. He's seen me."

"Oh Christ, no! Another hidin'," said Hughie. Peter Currie thought quickly. "We can say we've been workin down here."

"Aye, say that – hic," said Hughie, "It's not really a bad lie. We did some – hic – tidyin' yesterday. Wipe your mouth Johnnie, ye've some meal round it." They all wiped their mouths.

Again Currie put his head above the coaming, to be confronted with the dark greatcoat of the Mate.

"I thought you were supposed tae be workin' on deck," said Kerr, allowing Currie to climb out on to the deck but clipping John round the head as he emerged.

"We'd done it all, sir," said Currie, "so we thought we'd finish up some tidyin' below an' get a little warm too."

"Oh yes?" The Mate's tone condemned them, "Let's have a look shall we? Go down and show me what you've done."

Hughie went red and bit his lip as he descended. In the hold John and Peter Currie showed the Mate the tidying that had been done the previous day. This, to their surprise, seemed to satisfy him.

"Alright, up ye go," he said, with almost a hint of disappointment in his voice. The boys climbed to the half deck and quickly began their ascent to open air.

"Wait a minute…" said Kerr, as his head appeared above the half deck, "what's this?"

The boys stopped on the ladder, their hearts sinking.

"Come down now, and explain this away if ye can."

The boys gathered round the offending cask with looks of astonishment on their faces.

"Come on. What's this?"

"Looks like meal Sir," said Hughie.

"Don't play the innocents wi' me. I thought it was strange, you lot doin' work ye weren't made tae do. Ye's common thieves the lot o' ye. Wait here. I'm gettin' the Captain." Hughie was quaking with fear as Kerr returned with the Captain.

"Claimed they were cleanin' up down here – look what I found."

"I will not have stealin' on board this ship!" spat Captain Watt.

"We didn't…" pleaded three voices as one.

Watt interrupted. "Mister Nobody, was it? We'll see if a good rope endin'll gi'us a culprit."

He grabbed Hughie by the arm and jerked him towards the ladder.

"It wasnae me," wailed the boy, in floods of tears.

"Go and wait by the sail room," Watt ordered. "You two as well."

John and Peter Currie followed on.

"Fetch Bryson, Brand and McGinnes. They can have a rope's end too."

"Aye Sir," said Kerr. "Not Reilly?"

"Yes, him too." The stowaways were lined up with their hands resting against the poop bulkhead. Kerr dealt out the punishment of three lashes each, smiling as he did so. The boys were not asked to strip and the punishment did little real damage through several layers of clothing.

"I hope ye've learned Ye's lesson," said the Captain.

"It's not fair!" John shouted, "It wasna us, it was the crew."

The Captain paused.

"Aye, it was. We heard them," added Hughie.

"I don't believe ye," said Watt, turning away in a pretence of disinterest. Unusually for him, Currie shouted, "I swear to God it was. I saw them. I swear on my mother's life."

There was something in Currie's voice that Captain Watt could not dismiss. He turned and aimed a threatening finger.

"If you're lyin' I'll have ye beaten within an inch of your lives."

"We're *not* lyin'," said John.

Captain Watt walked up to Currie. The boy drew back, rubbing his arm and sniffing.

"Ye can identify the man who took the meal?" asked the Captain.

"I saw one of them" said Currie, his voice returning to its usual quiet tone. Watt turned to Kerr who had been standing silently in the shadows.

"Mister Kerr," he said, "turn out the off duty watch and have the whole crew assemble on deck."

It seemed odd to John to see so many of the crew at one time. Captain Watt called Currie forward.

"Point out the man you saw." The boy's eyes scanned the group. It was difficult. He had only caught a glimpse of the man in strong light from above. It could have been any one of four of the seamen. He flushed and began to whimper as he could see his failure turning into severe beatings for all. And what would Bryson do to him?

A sudden tilt of the head by one of the crew made the boy certain.

"It was him," said Currie, pointing an unsteady finger.

"Manson? I find that hard tae believe. Are ye certain?" asked the Captain.

"Aye Sir," said Currie, as firmly as he could. Manson, red faced, protested his innocence.

"It's a mistake. It wasnae me. Honest Sir."

"Mister Kerr," said Watt with dignity, "take Hendry wi'ye and search the fo'c's'le."

"Aye Sir."

As the two men made for the bow of the ship, the remainder waited. The Captain ordered some of the crew back to their duties but the rest were kept, shivering and stepping from foot to foot, on deck. The Captain paced in preoccupied impatience. Before long Kerr and Hendry returned to the assembly; Hendry was carrying some plump bags.

"Found these in the Fo'c's'le, Sir, in Mitchell Manson's and Miller Crabbie's chests, so it looks like the brats are tellin' the truth for a change."

"Manson. I'm surprised at you. I thought you were worth more than that," said The Captain. The seaman hung his head. Kerr added, "Ye aren't men at all tae see these boys flogged for what you have done."

"I'm sorry Sir," he muttered.

The Captain's voice was irritable. "Crabbie led ye into it, no doubt. Get over here now, the pair o' ye. The rest o' ye get back tae your duties."

The crew drifted away silently.

"Mister Kerr, we'll have both o' them in irons. Chain 'em to a stanchion on the poop." His eyes fell on Currie and John who were smiling knowingly at one another. Watt wondered if he had been manipulated and felt his anger rising. "As for you brats..." – the boys' smiles dropped to the deck – "I expect you were helpin' y'sels too."

"We weren't," said John.

"Shut up boy. Speak when ye's bidden an' not before." He calmed his voice. "Mister Kerr, I want all the stowaways cuffed too. I want 'em kept out o' mischief. They can go up tae the fo'c's'le head. I want 'em tae call out every minute 'Ice ahead, all's well' – understand?"

"Tha's not fair Sir, we…" John began.

"Shut up!" said the Captain, surprising himself by lunging forward and giving the boy a back handed swipe across the face. John went sprawling to the deck and doubled up, clutching a mouth oozing red.

"Ye never learn do ye?" said Watt, his emotions a confused mix of anger, uncertainty and guilt. "Take 'em away Mister Kerr."

"Sir?" said Kerr his voice quiet and calm, "Can I speak wi' ye?" He drew the officer a little away from the boys and spoke in a hushed voice. "As Currie helped us to find the culprit perhaps we shouldn't punish him, and I really need Reilly and Brand tae help wi' the ship, wi Crabbie an' Manson out o' it."

"Alright then, iron the rest. Keep them there 'til eight." He looked at the stowaways. John was hunched and still holding his mouth, with Hughie and Jimmy attending to him. Only Bryson looked briefly in his direction. There was hatred in his glance.

"Keep Bryson there 'til midnight."

"Aye Sir."

Bryson, who had been unaware of the incident in the hold, being aft at the time, didn't take kindly to being ironed along with the others.

"Why? This isn't bloody fair. I want tae see the Captain," he said to the steward, who was chaining their hands behind their backs.

"I'd shut up if I were you," he said, "You're likely tae get a good beatin' for your trouble. The Master's in no mood, I can tell ye."

The small boys were chained together. Bryson was chained separately, hands, again, behind his back.

None of the stowaways enjoyed working in the cold, but at least the activity helped warm them a little. The enforced inactivity on the exposed forecastle head had them quaking and huddling together in an attempt to keep warm.

"I can't hear ye callin' out as ye were told," said Boatswain Thomson.

"Oh for Christ's sake," murmured Bryson, who then shouted as loud as he could, "Ice ahead, all's well!" as much to vent his anger as for any other reason. The boatswain chuckled and sauntered off, burying his hands deeper into his coat pockets.

Bryson was brooding; it was obvious from his expression. John noticed that he kept clenching his teeth, tightening the muscles in his cheeks. Finally he spoke.

"Currie was wi' ye in the hold, wasn't he?"

"Aye," answered Hughie.

"And Jimmy and me weren't. Yet we're put in irons an' he isn't. An' you say there's no funny business goin on?"

The boys looked at one another.

"He did say who stole the meal," said John.

"Yeah, a proper little saint, ain't he? He's poison. Take no notice o' his wide-eyed innocence. He'll do frae us all, given time. You see if he won't…"

## 20. *Chains, a meal and a wash*

To the boys and Bryson, inactive and chilled to the bone, the day seemed interminable. Their boredom was only relieved by the sighting of several ships, some sailing a similar course, others passing in the opposite direction.

There was still no sign of land, but occasionally gulls would punctuate the barren grey of the sky, their desolate cries cutting through the rush and creak of sea and ship.

Towards the middle of the afternoon, the Arran approached a fishing smack which was bobbing, almost jauntily, in a similar direction. Her single mast was rigged fore and aft with greatly patched brown sails. She was dwarfed by the Arran and was in a generally poor state.

Captain Watt ordered that the Arran be hove to. The smack did likewise, with a great flapping of sails as they spilled the wind. He then sent a boat loaded with a barrel of salt beef over to the old rust stained wooden vessel.

John looked at the smack and thought how scarred and lined it looked, showing its experiences and hardships. Curiously, its worn and rugged features reminded him of some of the old Greenock seamen, who drank and swapped tales in the quayside inns.

A deal was done and the barrel hauled on board the smack. In exchange bucketfuls of slithering silver were cascaded into the boat, to the outcry of a halo of dipping and weaving gulls.

"Look at that," said John. "I could eat that boat load on my own."

"And me," added Hughie.

"I bet we won't see much o' it," Bryson grumbled.

The light drained slowly from the sky. It became colder still and began to snow. The wind frothed the crests of the waves, and periodic icy and salty mists mingled with the gradually whitening decks. All the stowaways were now wet through and suffering badly.

"I'm not puttin' up wi' this much longer," said Bryson.

"What ye gonna do then?" asked Jimmy.

"Take shelter, stupid. I'll risk a lash or two."

John pleaded with him. "Oh, don't make trouble for us, we're sufferin' too."

"You can suffer all night if ye want. I'm buggered if I'm goin' to take much more o' it." He scanned the decks for signs of the ship's officers. He knew Kerr and the Captain were below. It was the boatswain's watch. Thus far, he had not had much to do with Thomson, but he didn't fear him.

He began pacing up and down the forecastle head, trying to see how he could, with hands chained behind his back and, with the motion of the ship, negotiate the steep steps to the deck without falling.

A greatcoated figure, hunched against the driving snow approached the forecastle. Bryson retired back to the huddled group of boys.

"Right, you little ones, ye can go tae the sailroom now," said the figure – it was Boatswain Thomson. The boys needed no further encouragement but shuffled stiffly towards the steps.

"We can't get down," said Hughie. "Our hands are tied."

"Jump down. Ye'd do it in Well Park wouldn't ye? Just jump. I'll catch ye if ye fall." Thomson sounded almost genial.

"After three," said John, and on the three the trio of boys jumped and landed in a heap and a flurry of snow. Hughie complained that the iron manacles had hurt his wrist and he cried a little. Bryson jumped down too when he thought Thomson's attention was elsewhere, but the careful drop to the deck ended as a skid, and a foot stamped on the deck as he tried to keep his feet.

"And where d'ye think you're goin?" said Thomson.

"If they can go tae the sail room, so can I."

"No you can't. Get back on to the fo'c's'le. You're tae bide there 'til midnight."

"Midnight! Bollocks tae that. I'm gettin out o' the weather too."

"You're not – get back up on the fo'c's'le, now."

"You gonna make me?" said Bryson. Thomson stood in his way.

"If I have tae I will."

"Go boil your head," said Bryson as he tried to push past the boatswain. Thomson checked the youth and pushed him sideways. Bryson lost his balance, slipped on the snow and, being unable to use his hands to check his fall, landed heavily across the anchor chains where they emerged from under the forecastle head. His face struck one of the heavy, unyielding links and his mouth gushed blood.

"Bastard!" he spat, speckling the snow with red. Thomson, his temper lost, kicked at Bryson's head, dashing it again on to the heavy chain. Still angry, but unaware at that moment of the damage he had done to Bryson, he dragged the groaning youth to his feet. He was shocked at the bloodied face, but did not soften.

"Now get back tae the fo'c's'le like ye's told." He pushed the stunned stowaway forward and Bryson staggered to the foot of the steps to the higher deck.

"I can't get up tae the deck wi'out my hands," his voice was breaking with desperation.

Thomson, his anger spent, sighed and helped Bryson up to the deck. Despite the conflict between them, he felt sorry for the defeated youth. Bryson's mouth and chin were wet with blood and a red rivulet ran from a cut and swollen eyebrow, to mingle with the tears which ran down his cheek.

Thomson went about his business and half an hour later returned. At first, he thought that Bryson had left the forecastle head and his anger began to rise. He swore under his breath and clenched his gloved fists tightly, but then he noticed a rounded form in the lee of the capstan.

Bryson's back, head and arms were cloaked in snow. His knees were drawn up to his chest and his head was rested on them. He was quaking, in periodic spasms, from head to foot.

The boys, still chained, but in the comparative warmth of the sailroom, heard a sound outside the door. Presently it opened and the cook came in, bearing a tin bowl which was steaming.

"Don't get excited," he said, putting it on the deck between them. He retrieved some spoons from his pocket and clattered them noisily alongside.

"Wha's that?" asked Jimmy, eyeing the bowl of black sludge suspiciously.

"Looks 'orrible," said John.

"Smells a bit like coffee," added Hughie.

The cook chuckled. "Hughie wins the prize! Your supper is coffee grounds and tea leaves."

"What kind o' meal is that?" asked John.

"The only one ye'll get tonight," said Salton.

"Nothin' else – No biscuit?"

"No, that's it. Mister Kerr locked everythin' else away."

As he was speaking, Currie, Brand and Reilly were ushered in and the boatswain, who followed, chained them, again behind their backs, to the other boys.

"Why are we bein' locked up like animals?" asked Reilly. "Sure we's done nothin' but work bloody hard all day."

"I just do as I'm told," said Thomson wearily. "If Mister Kerr says iron ye, I iron ye. If he says unlock ye, I do so. If ye've any complaints gi' em tae Mister Kerr or the Captain."

He left. The stowaways looked at one another. Brand shrugged his shoulders.

"How am I supposed to eat this wi' both hands behind my back?" Only the end boys; Hughie and Jimmy had one hand free.

"Youse'll have to feed us," said Reilly, "youse end boys."

The six shuffled close to the pot and were fed the unappetising gruel by the end two. Jimmy was at the left hand end and had only his left hand free. At first he found it difficult to use the spoon in the unfamiliar hand and his efforts, using a much too full spoon, decorated rather than fed his fellow stowaways. The expression of intensity on his face, his brow lifted, his small eyes wide with concentration and his mouth opening and shutting, as if willing the wobbling, dripping spoonful into the recipient's mouth, amused John so much that, having just been fed, he snorted in laughter, then nearly choked as the gritty sludge went backwards and up his nose.

It may have lacked nourishment, but the meal was plentiful and hot, and the stowaways felt warmed and satisfied, despite the dry, tannic aftertaste that lingered on. They all fell asleep and were unaware of Bryson's arrival at midnight, having been finally stood down. He was chained independently to an iron ring in the sail room.

His cheek, eyebrow and mouth were bruised and badly swollen, and caked blood was smeared over nearly all his face. As the boatswain left, Bryson watched him go, his eyes glowing with hate.

"Bastard!" he muttered as the warmly-clad figure disappeared into falling snow.

Snow fell all night, thickly blanketing the decks and the deckhouse roofs. As usual, the stowaways were roused at four and, in the light of a lamp, their manacles were removed. It was in this light that Brand noticed Bryson's face and the red-brown stains on his shirt front.

"Good God, what the hell's happened tae you?"

"Bloody Bo'sun worked me over. Me wi' me hands chained."

"Why, what did ye do tae deserve that?"

Tears began to form in Bryson's eyes. "I only wanted tae get out o' the cold," he whimpered.

Just then, Bosun Thomson came up to the group. "Brand, clean Bryson up will ye?" He turned to Bryson. "Sorry lad. I didna mean tae hurt ye so bad."

Bryson scowled. "Sorry? I bet ye are."

Thomson ignored him and walked off.

"Come on then James," said Brand, "let's clean ye up."

Besides his facial injuries, Bryson had cuts and bruising to his wrists where the manacles had dug in. The ones on his left wrist were quite deep.

"Jesus!" said Reilly, the cold wind stinging his face, "Is it ever goin' to warm up?" The ship's lights flickered as they made their way over the sloping deck. The snow, now inches deep in parts with deeper drifts here and there, covered a thin layer of ice, which the stowaways found quite treacherous. Keeping their footing on the deck was not easy and first Hughie, then Reilly, slipped and fell. All walked cautiously as if on eggshells.

Kerr, already on deck, ordered the stowaways to help the crew clear the snow and ice. Progress was slow and by daybreak only a small area of deck had been cleared. To make things worse, snow was again falling to veil the cleared deck timbers.

The stowaways were wearing all the clothes that they had. Hats and caps were pulled down, borrowed and improvised scarves, and turned up coat collars bridged the gap, leaving only as much flesh exposed as was needed to see where they were going. Moist, clouded breath froze on the cloth around their mouths and the sting of the wind watered their eyes and made their skin red and sore.

They worked for most of the day on clearing the snow from the decks. As a reddish tinge coloured the grey of the horizon as the light faded Kerr, warmly clad, came up and spoke to Hughie and John who were spading the snow over the side.

"Ye's workin' well lads. Keep that up an' I'll see what I can do for ye." He could see that Hughie was finding it hard work, each spadeful seemed to demand a lot of effort.

The Mate looked at Hughie. His red eyes were streaming in the cold and tears had washed clean pink tracks down his face. He pulled down the boy's collar and saw how dirty his face was.

"Good God boy, your face is filthy, when did ye last have a wash?"

"It's been so cold," replied Hughie, his chin trembling.

"I told ye tae keep y'sels clean. Reilly and Brand do, why can't you?" He exposed John's face to reveal a similarly grubby skin.

"Both of ye – go aft tae the sailroom and wait for me." The boys slipped and skidded their way back to the deck cabin.

"Let's wait inside," said John. Hughie didn't argue.

It wasn't long before a sailor entered.

"C'mon, Mister Kerr wants ye." They followed the man to the main hatch where Jimmy and Bryson were already removing their clothes.

"Oh no, not another scrubbin'," said Hughie, looking at their goose pimpled bodies and feeling suddenly colder.

"Clothes off lads," said Kerr breezily. The boys complied silently, feeling their own goose pimples rise as the biting wind scoured their nakedness. Reilly and Brand were stood nearby. John noted that they were fully dressed, but held soft brushes. One of the seamen collected their underclothes, shirts and trousers and each boy's clothes were made into a bundle, secured on to the end of a line of rope. These bundles were lowered overboard and into the black sea. This activity took place on the port side of the vessel and all the boys were watching.

A sudden pail of seawater dashed against their unsuspecting backs. All leaped forward, backs hollow and taut, as if they had been stabbed. A second bucketful delivered by a sailor from another direction dashed against their vulnerable bodies. Several of the seamen were watching and laughed as the stowaways gasped for breath.

"Start the scrubbin'," ordered Kerr.

"Sorry about this…" murmured Brand to Bryson, "I'll be as gentle as I can." He noted the fading weals and bruises and frowned. But Bryson was baring clenched teeth and was shaking in his battle with the cold. He didn't hear Brand. The abrasive wind felt red hot in its coldness on the boy's bodies and all were shivering uncontrollably. John and Hughie were crying. Hendry, one of the young seamen, was shovelling snow on the poop Kerr saw him and had an idea.

"Ever been tae Finland, any of ye?"

"No Sir" came the answer.

"Ah well, as a taster in case ye might go later, I'll introduce ye to the Finnish custom. All o' ye, get back by the poop rail - now."

The boys, with skin as white as marble, but blotchily pink where the brush had scoured, skidded and tottered to the poop bulkhead.

"Kneel down, just where ye are." The boys looked at one another wondering what was to come next. Kerr motioned to Hendry to shovel the snow on to the deck below.

To the Mate's delight they all called out as the shovelfuls of snow rained down on them.

"Come on," laughed Kerr, "rub y'sels wi' the snow, the Finns do it. Go on, put some effort into it, it'll do ye good."

Reluctantly, the boys took fistfuls of snow and rubbed themselves. Curiously, this did not feel as chilling as the wind did on their wet bodies. Further snow was brushed on to them from the poop, to the laughter of nearby crew members.

"Oh look, snowaways," joked one. Others groaned their appreciation. Another sailor threw a handful of snow which, a little off course, struck Bryson's thigh.

"Snowballs!" he said, to more laughter and groans. Bryson flashed a look in the direction from where the missile had come. His lips were clenched tightly.

"Put some effort in," repeated the Mate harshly. He looked at Bryson's swollen face and spoke quietly to him.

"Bryson?" The youth looked towards the officer. His former defiant attitude melted into one of fear. This was noted with satisfaction by the Mate.

"The face – it's a great improvement." He smiled at the youth's discomfiture and, to complete the humiliation, made a point of looking at Bryson's naked genitals, sneering his contempt.

"Snowballs." he chuckled, then quickly raised his voice and spoke to the stowaways as a whole.

"Ye've worked well today, for a change, so I'll gi' ye a biscuit each. Ye can go tae the sailroom tonight. Take your coats, I'll not need ye 'til mornin'."

## 21. Into the ice

The Arran was clearly finding progress through the encroaching ice difficult. The floes were becoming larger and closer together. Now and again the ship would veer off course, deflected by a particularly solid pan of ice, causing it to shudder and rock in the water.

On a couple of occasions, the ship almost stopped dead. During one of these incidents a sailor, John Bruce, who had begun his climb aloft, was injured when he was catapulted from the shrouds to the deck. The Arran was now moving at a painfully slow pace and the character of the ice floes was changing. The initial thin, flat pans were now replaced by thicker, more irregular surfaced floes, some resembling small icebergs. Some were formed by thinner pans being forced one on top of the other; some had tilted at an angle and many of the larger pans had shallow turquoise lakes within them.

After looking over the side at the new scarring of the ship's hull, Captain Watt organised the crew to take spare hatch covers, gratings, barrels, spars and rope mats, and suspend them around the ship to fend off the ice from the hull. By nightfall the ship had stopped, finally trapped in the ice. The sails were clewed up and the ship was quiet, apart from the mournful whine of the wind through the rigging.

The sky was a dirty backdrop to the pale greens and blues, which gave form to the brilliant white ice field.

John and Hughie were helping a seaman coil some ropes when John noticed a brig sailing some distance away, clear of the ice but on their heading. She seemed to be making good speed. He looked around before whispering to his friend.

"I reckon we've got a rotten Master, tae be stuck like this. Look at that ship – she's goin' like a train – full sail. We could be stuck here for ever."

He was overheard by the seaman, who lost no time in putting the boy right.

"That brig's about half our draught. We have tae stay tae the channel no matter what. If we did as she's doin' we'd be aground in no time." He left the two boys to their task.

A shaft of strong light illuminated a grey, humped form on the horizon. It drew John's eye: it was faint, but there was no doubt, it was land, rising steeply from the sea. Almost as soon as it became visible, the clouds closed up and it was gone.

"Did you see that?" asked John.

"What?" asked his friend.

"Land. I saw land."

"Where?" he craned his head to look in the same direction as John. "Where y' lookin'?"

"On the horizon, it was like cliffs. It's gone now."

"If it was there just now, how can it be gone?"

"I don't know but it was definitely land."

"You thought it was land last time and it wasna'."

"That was different, this wasna' cloud."

"I bet it was."

"Bet it wasna' – bet ye a farthin'."

"Ye havena' got a farthin'."

"Alright then, I bet ye half a bag o' meal."

"Ye havena' got any meal."

"I have so."

"Show me it then."

John took a bulky, cloth-covered package from his pocket, unwrapped it carefully and showed Hughie its contents.

"Where d'ye get that?" he asked.

"Found it in the hold."

"Is there any more?"

"No, this is all I found, wrapped just as ye see. Looks like a bit o' flag."

Hughie thought for a moment.

"Alright then, I'll bet ye."

"What ye got tae bet wi'?" asked John.

"I'll get somethin'."

John re-tied the flag around the meal.

"Och, no deal, you ain't got nothin'."

"I'll get somethin'."

A sudden voice behind them made them jump.

"What ye doin'?" said Currie. John tried to discreetly replace the meal in his pocket but the newcomer noticed it.

"What ye got there, Johnnie?" With resignation, after first looking around to see that no-one was coming, John pulled the package from his pocket, untied the knot and showed the boy,

"Don't tell anyone, will ye? There's not that much as it is."

"Where d'ye get it?"

"I found it in the hold."

"I wonder who put it there?" asked Currie.

"Perhaps it's a trap," said Hughie, "P'raps they wanted us tae find it. P'raps it was put there so as we would find it and eat it."

"Perhaps its poisoned!" exclaimed Currie.

John ignored this and spoke to Hughie. "Why would anyone try tae trap us?"

"Tae get us in trouble again – could be those two that Peter told on, gettin their own back on us."

John looked thoughtfully into Hughie's eyes.

"It is odd tae find it wrapped like that," he looked down at the package, "in such a bright coloured bit o' flag." All three eyed the package suspiciously.

"Perhaps we should throw it overboard," said Peter Currie.

"No, I think we should gi' it tae Mister Kerr. We can tell him how I found it. If it was put there tae catch us out it won't work, if we hand it in."

"You can gi' it him then… I'm buggered if I will!" said Hughie.

"I don't think I'm the one tae gi' it him either. Peter's the best one – seein' as he knows him."

"Me?" exclaimed Currie.

"Ye've only tae gi' it him," said Hughie lightly.

John carefully re-tied the package and gave it to the boy. Currie looked from John to Hughie and then at the package.

"Oh, alright then," he said.

"He's on the poop," said Hughie.

"See you later," said John.

Currie looked again at both John and Hughie before beginning his lonely walk to the poop. Ten yards on he stopped and turned.

"Come wi' us," he pleaded.

The two boys looked at one another.

"Oh, please come wi' me. I won't go unless ye do."

The two boys, at a slight distance, followed Currie along the slippery deck. Kerr was at the poop rail. His face was flushed and there was a metal flask in his hand. He saw the boys approach and turned his back on them.

"Sir?" said Currie nervously, circling the Mate, holding the parcel in front of him like a precious offering.

"Aye…" replied Kerr irritably.

"Please Sir, we found this in the hold."

"What is it?" Currie opened it to reveal the contents. Before he had time to react he was grabbed by the scruff of the neck and dragged to the poop steps. The meal flew in all directions.

As soon as they saw the Mate's reaction John and Hughie beat a hasty retreat, to hide behind a deckhouse. They peered round the edge to see a wailing Currie pushed from the poop to fall awkwardly on to the main deck.

"Go and get the rest of the stowaways, now!" shouted Kerr, his eyes wide and white against the crimson of his face.

All the stowaways came to the poop apart from Reilly. Hughie began coughing and had one hand clasped to his chest.

"Where's the Irishman?" asked the Mate.

"Workin aloft wi' a couple o' the seamen, Sir." said Brand.

"Aye, well, he'll keep" He took a rope from the rail and drew it through his hand.

"Alright then… hands against the poop bulwark."

"Whose idea was this?" said Hughie, his voice congested and a smear of blood on his mouth.

"I'm gettin' a thrashin' too," said John. "I thought he'd be pleased we told."

"Should ha' thrown the stuff overboard like I said," grumbled Currie to no-one in particular.

"Sir, this really isna' fair," said Brand, "We've done nothin' wrong. Is this what we get for bein' honest?"

The Mate's response was to punch Brand hard in the face. He reeled backwards. His lips, already dried and cracked by the cold, bled profusely, but being numb with cold he felt no sensation of pain.

"I'll have nae more o' yer cheek. Now turn round like you were told." Brand put his hands on the bulkhead and clenched his teeth in anticipation of the lashes. The rope cracked twice across his back.

Next to suffer the rope was Bryson who, from the sound of it, was given harder blows. The youth drew sharp breaths after each of the lashes and clenched white-knuckled fists.

Jimmy was trembling, sobbing and muttering to himself.

"Wha's the matter wi' you?" asked Kerr.

"Nothin'," sobbed the boy.

The Mate turned the boy's face towards his own.

"What ye greetin' for?"

"I wish I'd never come. I want tae go home . I want my Ma."

"I wish ye could go home. I didna' invite ye here in the first place. Turn ye's back."

He was given two less severe lashes with the rope. All the small boys were crying but received their lashes without complaint. Hughie was coughing again. John was surprised that the lashes had not hurt more. The coat he wore had absorbed much of the power of the blows and the cold further dulled the sensation.

"Ye can get tae the fo'c's'le now. I'll have the steward chain ye again."

The wind dropped, the temperature rose and gradually the roof of cloud slid away to reveal a clear blue sky and the smile of the sun. Land could now be clearly seen on the horizon, rising sharply from the sea.

The fringe of ice around the deckhouse roofs began to melt and occasionally lumps dropped to smash like glass on the deck. The ship's sails were now neatly brailed upon their yards and there was little for the crew to do other than maintenance work.

The sound of voices and laughter could be heard by the stowaways, coming from the forecastle beneath their feet. Despite the change in the weather, it was still cold and the jollity below only seemed to make them feel more miserable.

Again, the stowaways were told to call out "Ice ahead, all's well" every five minutes, but they only did this when an officer was about.

John thought that 'ice ahead' was less than truthful for, indeed, ice was all around – since being trapped the ice field had extended. The pans were large and irregular in shape. They creaked and groaned with the movements of the sea beneath and occasional explosions of ice occurred as pans were pressed tightly against one another.

As the day warmed a new sound was heard by Hughie.

"I can hear a dog barkin'."

"Dogs, out here? Ye must be barmy," said Bryson.

"Shh, there it is again... listen..."

They all listened. Hughie was right, there was a faint barking sound, then another, a little closer.

"Over there, look," said Jimmy, pointing.

"What?" said Brand.

"Dunno but it was dark and it was slidin along."

"A seal?" asked Bryson.

"Could be."

"They make a noise like a bark," added Brand.

Suddenly a dark shape forty yards away emerged from the glaring white of the ice. It was a seal. It looked around, studying the Arran carefully, before flopping away behind some large lumps of ice, to re-emerge the other side and slide down into the white like a rabbit going down its burrow.

The remainder of the day passed uneventfully. The stowaways watched small craft sailing by, beyond the ice's ragged fringe, but the ice field itself was moving, drawing the Arran further into St Georges Bay.

The movement of the ice pans gradually turned the ship until by late afternoon it was moving backwards towards the land.

That evening the smell of fish cooking met the hungry stowaways' nostrils and at eight o' clock when they went off watch, a steaming cauldron of fish broth was placed on the hatch cover for them to eat. This thin soup was made from the heads, tails and bones of the fish which had been traded earlier. A little meal had been added to thicken it.

The crew watched the ravenous stowaways squabbling and jostling for position around the pot, each fighting to spoon as much as he could of the grey liquid. Currie and Jimmy found it difficult to get past the barricade of jerking elbows and consequently didn't get much. Currie wasn't too concerned because he was receiving bits and pieces on the sly from other sources, but it was different for Jimmy, whose stomach ached with anticipation. In the end only his tearful pleas opened a place for him.

It was while stretching over the cauldron, his face wet with condensed steam, that John noticed a tearing sound and felt a sudden chill to his buttocks. There was much laughter among the crew behind him.

"Ye's feedin' 'em too much Sir," said a seaman to Kerr, "they're burstin' outa their breeches!" More laughter ensued.

When the meal was over and Jimmy was left alone, picking bits of skin from the bones at the bottom of the cauldron, John sought out the Steward.

"Mister McLean Sir," he said when he found him. "I've put me arse outa me trousers, Sir, have ye a spare pair I can have?"

"Come wi' me," said McLean gruffly.

They walked along to the sail room, where the Steward, after rummaging in a corner produced what John imagined was a neatly folded pair of buff canvas trousers. His smile faded as he unfolded the 'trousers' to find that it was just a piece of canvas.

"I've no trousers tae fit a wee sprat like you, laddie; but if ye's nice tae one o' the seamen, they may make ye up a new pair out o' that. John Bruce used to be good but he's no well, so yell have tae ask some o' the others."

John looked rather despondent.

"Have ye a needle an' thread, Sir?" he asked, "I'll try an' mend these until I can get the new ones made up.

McLean sighed and without comment turned and from a cupboard took a sailmaker's needle and a cop of hempen thread. Taking out his knife, he drew an arm's length of yarn from the reel and cut it off. He coiled it loosely around his fingers, and with the needle, held it in front of John's face.

"I want this needle back by tomorrow night, ye ken? – you are responsible for it – don't lose it."

"No, Sir. Er... Sir?"

"What now?"

"Can I mend 'em now – there's an awful draught an' me bum's gettin' cold."

McLean smiled. "Go on then, but don't be all day. I don't want Mister Kerr after me." He went to leave, but stopped in the doorway. "Ye can leave the needle on the sail over there when ye've finished. Stick it in the canvas then it won't get lost."

"Aye Sir – thank ye Sir."

When he removed his trousers he found that it was only the stitching of the seam that had gone. He began to sew up the seam in the same way that he had seen his mother do it. He was in no hurry to go out again into the cold and so worked slowly and carefully. The waxed thread was a little stiff but worked easily, and within a quarter of an hour he was finished. He removed the surplus thread by grinding it between his front teeth. The yarn was tough, but eventually weakened enough to break with his hands. He didn't put the trousers on straight away, but snatched a further quarter of an hour in the comparative warmth of the sail room.

A further visit from McLean ended his respite.

"Have ye done?"

"Aye, Sir, just finished this second." The Steward took the trousers and looked at the neat stitching.

"Very good work. Have tae get ye on sail mendin'."

John was surprised and pleased by the compliment, the first he'd received since coming on board the Arran.

"Thank ye, Sir. I'd like that."

"Aye, well tha's for the future. Now ye must get back tae ye's duties." John climbed into his trousers and bent over to test the stitching. They felt secure.

"Yes I'd like tae mend the sails, Sir." The cold wind tugged at his hair and clothes as he left the sail room. He shuddered. "I'd like that very much," he added. His thoughts continued the sentence. 'Anything tae get out o' this awful cold!'

## 22. *More ice*

As the tide took the Arran further into the Bay of St George the hill's snowy caps, pink in the morning light, became clearly visible, but still the distance was too great to make out any houses. The weather, although still cold, was tempered by occasional breaks in the cloud, which allowed the sun through.

A smell of paint drifted across the decks from the poop, where Bryson was rather listlessly painting the rails and stanchions with a new coat of white. He saw the Captain coming and worked more earnestly.

The youth was relieved when the officer passed him without a word, continuing to the rear of the poop and looking landwards through a telescope. Bryson watched him.

It was as if he was searching for something in particular. The telescope slowly described an arc from port to starboard. When this was complete he took it from his eye and stared at the land ahead, before looking down to the ice at the stern. It was at this point that Seaman Hendry approached him. He seemed irritated by the interruption to his train of thought.

"Sir?" said Hendry, touching the peak of his cap, "Can Hunter and me take a rifle and go shoot a few seals?"

"No," said Watt crossly, but Hendry pursued the matter.

"It'd mean fresh meat for us all, Sir."

"I said no and no I meant. The ice isn't sound enough yet – it might give way. I'm a man short as it is with Bruce out o' action. I don't want to lose two more from drownin'." His tone softened a little. "I'll think about it if the ice firms up a bit more."

"Aye Sir," said Hendry, leaving the Officer to resume his scanning of the distant land.

John was working with Hughie, scraping varnish from a spar which, from its size and fittings, John supposed to be a royal yard. The wood had blackened where water had got under the varnish. John found it quite satisfying when the varnish came off in large amber coloured flakes. He and Hughie had been told that if they made a good job of it they could re-varnish the yard – a job they were looking forward to as light relief from the sore fingers acquired from the seemingly endless scraping.

His stomach was aching – none of the stowaways had eaten since the fish broth the previous day – and he felt miserable. He looked at his right hand; the skin had cracked and bled on the side of his forefinger. The crack seemed to open and close as he moved his hand, but it was no longer bleeding. Anyway his hands were still too cold to have any feeling. They only came to in the relative warmth of the hold or sail locker, to complain eloquently of their abuse.

Hughie sniffed and John looked at him. He was crying. How tightly the waxy skin was stretched over the bones of his face, his wet eyes looked faded and his mouth, with pale cracked lips, was slightly open.

"Wha's the matter Hughie?" he said softly. The boy's sobs increased and he wiped the tears away with the heels of his hands. He sniffed.

"Nothin much; I just wish I wasna here. I wish I was back at school. I keep thinkin' I'm gonna wake up in a minute an' I'll be in me own bed, but the second I wake up I know its not a dream. I miss my Ma. I 'spect she's forgotten all about me by now. It's all your fault – talkin' me into comin'."

"I didna talk ye intae it – ye wanted tae come."

"You said it was gonna be fun."

"I thought it would be." John put his arm round his friend's shoulder and shook him gently. "Come on Hughie, we'll soon be outa this. We're nearly there. We'll look back an' laugh, you see if we don't." John affected a smile but this began to crumble as he, too, began to cry. Through the distortion of his tears he saw someone moving on deck. He blinked and saw the cook leave the galley with a bucket, which he emptied over the side. John jumped up and ran to the rail hoisting himself up to look over.

"Hughie," he called.

"What?" came the unenthusiastic reply.

"Cook's thrown some grub overboard – it's on the ice. The ladder's down. I'll go and get it. We can share it."

He clambered over the rail. The rope ladder swung and swayed as he made a nervous descent to the ice, chest pressed tightly to the flat treads as he went.

He carefully tested the ice before letting go of the ladder. It was cold and sharp against the soles of his feet and felt insecure, moving with the water currents. Edging gingerly away from the ladder he made his way to the potato peelings, put some in his mouth and crammed as many as he could into his cap. Balancing carefully, like a tightrope walker, he made his way back to the ship and lunged for the safety of the ladder. He was surprised that the ice was not smooth. It had gravel-sized bits of ice frozen into its surface. These made walking uncomfortable. Where it was smooth it was slippery under the thin veil of snow.

Climbing the ladder was impossible with the cap in one hand. After a second or two of thought he stuffed the cap and its contents into the front of his coat. Hughie was waiting for him at the top of the ladder and together they scurried off to consume the booty in the privacy of the sail room.

Bryson and Brand were there and they all crunched the skins eagerly, seemingly ignorant of the gritty clay that clung to some of them.

❖ ❖ ❖

"How far d'ye reckon it is tae land," Captain Watt asked, standing at the stern rail and looking towards the vague hills in the distance.

"Eight to ten miles I reckon; perhaps a little more," answered Kerr.

"Yes, I thought about ten," Watt again looked through his telescope.

"I can see houses. If we get a bit closer to land we could get the stowboys to walk ashore."

Kerr was surprised at this statement and felt uneasy.

"Send them ashore?"

"Aye, I thought ye'd like the idea."

"Yes – get rid o' em." But his voiced enthusiasm was a mask for his doubts. He looked at the ice – it was still in separate floes rather than in a solid sheet.

"The ice isnae good enough yet," he said.

"No, but give it a couple o' days. It's firmin' up all the time.

Kerr looked at the distant shadowy hills. It was an awfully long way, and even if the ice did firm up how could they be sure that it went to the shore. What if they were stranded on the ice?

'Why am I worrying about that lot,' he thought, trying to reason away his unease. 'They're strong enough tae make it. Eight miles – tha's nothin' if the ice is sound. Hardly more than a stroll.' But his doubts returned. 'What if they don't make it? What if they all drown – so what if they did? Who would miss 'em?' For a moment this satisfied him, but the doubts would not go away. 'What if some o' them die and some make land – what then?' He chided himself. 'What if – what if. What am I worried about?' This mental bravado didn't work.

"Perhaps we should keep the brats on board. After all, we've brought 'em this far."

"What? You really surprise me James," said the Captain, "I thought you'd be happy tae be rid o' 'em."

"Aye, I would – but they seem better lately – the beatin's helped tae bring 'em into line."

"Ah well, we'll see – we could be in the ice for a few weeks yet."

Later Kerr climbed to the main cross tree and looked out across the ice to the land. He had taken a telescope and he scanned the ice between ship and shore. It appeared more solid the further it went into the bay, and seemed to go to the shore. This reassured him somewhat, but the ice a half mile or so from the ship was still broken and in separate pans. It would not be long though – the ice was becoming more solid by the hour.

He decided to try a small experiment and walked quietly up behind Bryson, who was bent forwards painting the lower part of one of the rail stanchions. He whacked him across the buttocks with the flat of his hand. This made the youth jump and he banged his head on the underside of the rail. He grimaced and held his head, swearing under his breath. Kerr smiled.

"I want you and the other stowboys here by the rail now." He noted seaman Hunter a distance along the deck.

"Hunter…"

"Sir?"

"Here."

"Aye Sir."

As Bryson loped off, still rubbing his head and muttering to himself Hunter came up to the Mate.

"Here," said Kerr, putting his hand on the taller man's shoulder and whispering to him.

As John and Hughie arrived at the rail they saw the two men break away from their private discussion. Hunter appeared to be trying to restrain a smile and eventually turned his head away from the boys.

"Right lads," said the Mate brightly, "It's a nice day, so we're sendin' ye ashore. The ice goes right tae the land so ye'll have nae difficulties. 'Tis only a few miles o' walkin'. Ye'll be shown the way by Hunter here."

John looked at the sailor, who was still wrestling with the urge to laugh.

"Over the side ye go, now."

No-one moved, stunned by the idea.

"Sir, don't ye think…" began Brand.

"Just do as ye's told!" spat Kerr.

"Sir, I can hardly see…" Brand continued.

"Shut your mouth boy an' get over the side." He brandished a short end of rope and put his hand on Currie's shoulder to stop him.

"Not you laddie. I have a task for ye on board."

Currie blushed and cast a glance at Bryson, who looked back with a penetrating glare. Hunter, still smiling, led the group down the ladder. Bryson, Brand and Reilly followed on. Jimmy was climbing over and it was John's turn next. He hung back. Having had the feel of the ice beneath his feet he was not happy to repeat the experience. He turned to the Mate who, a second earlier had nudged him toward the rail.

"Sir, I don't feel well."

Tired of such excuses, Kerr again nudged the boy towards the rail.

"Go on Peacock, get on the ladder."

"No, no, I don't want tae go!"

The Mate grabbed him, shook him roughly and pushed him towards the rail. Almost hysterical, the boy struggled, broke free and ran off toward the forecastle.

"Come back here!" Kerr demanded, but before he could chase after the boy, his attention was taken by Hughie, who was also about to make off. The Mate grabbed him by the arm and swung him into the rail. "Get on to the ladder!" In tears, the boy complied.

John had hidden for an instant behind the fore deck house, but upon seeing the Mate turn his attention to Hughie, dashed under the forecastle head. From here he could see along the deck to where Kerr and a few seamen stood and also, through a hawser hole could see the stowaways on the ice watching Hughie's descent.

Hunter raised his arm, pointed toward the shore and led them away from the ship. The ice looked better from this vantage point than it had felt. Jimmy, barefoot like John, was obviously suffering as sharp ice gravel dug into the soles of his feet. Hughie looked back, no doubt in the hope of seeing his best friend. He was still crying. John felt more than a little guilty about escaping.

Hughie's boots slipped on the ice and he fell hard on his side. Now both he and Jimmy were wailing piteously. Hunter stopped, looked back and shouted at the young boys who were staggering along even more cautiously. He and the older youths waited for them to catch up. Bryson was clearly impatient to go on.

As a united group, they all resumed their journey, but it wasn't long before first Jimmy, then Bryson and Reilly slipped and fell over. Hughie slipped again but a degree of flapping of arms and Jimmy's assistance saved him.

The two small boys, clinging to one another, moved jerkily like marionettes, their feet shuffling along. They soon fell behind and sobbed loudly, pleading for the older ones to wait.

Again Hunter stopped, shouted at them and impatiently waited for them to catch up. When they reached him the group moved off at the speed of the slowest. Brand looped his arm through Hughie's and helped him along. They wove their way around difficult areas and over the joins between the pans of ice. The further they went the greater their confidence became.

They were about four hundred yards from the ship when Hunter stopped the group, said something to them and then set off back to the ship. The stowaways didn't seem concerned but watched him return. John peered along the line of the deck to see Kerr and a few others looking over the side. They were all laughing as Hunter came back on board. Much to John's surprise they pulled up the ladder, giving the stowaways no retreat. He heard the Mate say, "Well done Hunter, they really fell for it." They all laughed.

Brand heard their merriment and was angry. He started to run back to the ship, but slipped and fell, to raucous laughter from the watching crew. He swore, picked himself up and walked on.

"What the hell are ye doin!" he shouted, but they were not listening. From his hiding place, John could hear the laughter and make out the odd phrase.

"Go on, bugger off! Go an' play wi' the seals!"

"Good riddance!"

"Look at 'em slidin' about!"

Reilly and McGinnes came back to join Brand who was now close to the ship's side. A minute later Hughie tottered unsteadily up with arms outstretched to balance himself. Only Bryson waited, finally sauntering despondently back to the ship.

Brand would have dearly loved to have hurled abuse at the idiots who were putting them through this ordeal. It would have relieved the pent up anger which caused his hands to shake so. But he knew that would only heighten their merriment and probably prolong their stay on the ice.

"Can ye put the ladder down please," he asked firmly, trying to subdue the anger within him; anger which was becoming so hard to hide.

"We've finished wi' ye," said one sailor.

"Go drown y'sels," said another."

"I'm touched that ye want tae come back," said Kerr.

"They must be touched to want tae come back," said another, to renewed guffaws.

Reilly could see that Brand was on the point of losing control. He put his hand on the youth's arm.

"Easy, Davie," he said quietly, "I'll have a go." He looked up towards the rail. "This isn't fair on the wee ones, Have your fun wi' us if ye have to, but spare a thought for them. Poor McGinnes with no shoes."

He pointed at the boy who was still quietly crying. He had grazed his foot on the ice and was leaving a small pink stain of blood at every step. The laughter, although still there, seemed more forced than before.

Hughie was bent slightly, his arms still spread to balance himself. Even standing still was difficult as the worn hobnails gave no grip on the melting and irregular surface of the ice.

Brand's incipient fury had tempered itself into a cold resolve and as Kerr moved away from the group by the rail, making his way towards the poop, Brand followed by the others, shadowed him on the ice.

"Sir, please. Let us back on board. The little ones are really sufferin'. For pity's sake put down the ladder."

There was no response from Kerr, who looked resolutely in front of him.

"It's no much further tae Quebec. We'll be no more trouble, honest, Sir."

Kerr now stood with his back leaning against the poop rail, pretending not to hear their entreaties. Crew members still taunted them, throwing potato peelings and other refuse at them. A half hour later they had fallen silent, the crew had become bored and had gone from the rail. Only Kerr remained, his back still towards them. There seemed no way to reach this man. They had found no chink in the armour.

Hughie looked up at the solid high wooden walls of the Arran. The masts soared right up to the sky. The sails were furled neatly on top of their yards and only staysails were set to steady the ship.

A sudden slapping sound from aloft caused Kerr to look up. A sudden gust had filled these sails and caused the ship to move beam on in the water. A crunching sound and an explosion of fragmented ice announced the movement of the floes at the stern where the stowaways were. The pan on which Jimmy stood tipped alarmingly and as he jumped quickly on to another, this too moved. All the stowaways scrambled away from the cracking ice. The gust died and a gap of black water opened up between the ship and the lads.

"For pity's sake, we'll all be drowned!" shouted Reilly.

"Help us, please help us!" pleaded Jimmy.

"Put down the ladder!" ordered Kerr. The ladder was quickly lowered, but the lane of water and broken ice could not be crossed. Kerr disappeared from view and returned half a minute later.

"Come round the stern, quickly," he ordered. "The ice is all right there."

Gingerly skirting the stern, the stowaways found a place where they could approach the hull. The ladder was quickly lowered and they hastily climbed back on board.

John had lost sight of them when Kerr had gone aft. He had felt the ship move and heard the sound of the ice breaking up. But the sound of his friends' panic stricken voices had frightened him. He was relieved to see them, one by one, climb on to the deck. The two small boys were still crying and were almost rigid with cold.

He felt that it was now safe to come out of hiding. Jimmy was hobbling. His feet were blotchily grey and purple. He sat down on a hatch cover and tried to massage some feeling back into them. Kerr was looking at him.

"I can't feel my feet," sniffed the boy, examining the cut on the side of his foot, which by now had stopped bleeding, he licked his fingers and dabbed it, pressing the small flap of torn skin back into the wound.

Kerr clapped his hands. "Come on then – you've had your chance tae get away – if ye want tae stay ye can get back tae work. See Mister Niven, he'll give ye your tasks."

Jimmy's feet were coming round. It felt as if broken glass was in his veins as pain replaced numbness. He began to wail and hold his feet.

"God alive, what a pantomime," shouted Kerr, slapping the poop rail with his hands. "Either ye get tae work boy, or ye can go back on the ice."

Jimmy hobbled off in a somewhat theatrical way, hoping in vain to make Kerr feel some remorse for putting them on the ice.

Kerr looked out across the whiteness to the distant shore. 'The bigger brats could make it,' he thought, 'but I doubt that the wee ones would survive.'

## 23. *Another beating*

For most of the next day, cold, damp fog enveloped the Arran. Visibility was no more than thirty yards from the ship and the upper masts dissolved into it. The stowaways were all occupied on menial tasks. Most were on deck. Only Hughie and Currie were working below. John was paired with Jimmy. They were tidying ropes at the pinrail.

"You seem quiet today," said John.

" I don't feel too good. This cold – I don't think I can cope wi' much more o' it. Bein' stuck on the ice wi' no shoes yesterday didna' help either."

"I know. I've been down there too."

"Think I've got a wee chill, I feel rotten."

"Go see Mister Kerr – tell him – he might let ye off work."

"No fear."

"He could only say no."

"I wouldna ask. I don't need another beatin'. I just want tae keep out o' his way"

"But if ye's not well…"

"I think half the reason I feel rotten is because I'm so hungry. I got nothin' tae fight wi'."

John looked around – there was no-one near. He whispered to his companion. "Come wi' me. I got a stash o' meal."

"Where d'ye get that?"

"I promised I wouldna tell."

They scurried across the deck and down into the hold.

After a few secretive mouthfuls each, they began to climb the ladder to the deck. The sound of voices over their heads made them stop, then descend again into the dark safety of the hold. They listened intently. One of the voices was Reilly's.

"Sir, I have tried to be careful with what little food I'm given, but I must have more. I get the same amount as little Paul or McEwan. I'm sure you know how hard I work. I do my best but I do need more to eat. Could…"

A voice interrupted. It was the Captain's.

"The owners don't put provisions on board for stowaways. Count your blessings that you're fed at all." Reilly began to speak again, but was stopped by the Captain.

"If you're not happy wi' the feedin' arrangements ye can always leave the ship."

Reilly raised his hands, shrugged and, lost for an effective response, sighed.

"I'm sure ye have some work tae attend to," said the Captain coldly. "Don't let me keep ye."

When the voices had stopped, John crept up the ladder and cautiously peered over the edge of the hatch coaming. It seemed that the coast was clear so he and Jimmy climbed out onto the deck. A sudden voice behind them made them jump.

"And where have you two been?"

"Er… Had tae get somethin'," said John.

The Captain looked at Jimmy.

"Takes two o' ye does it?" He peered at the boy's face. "What's that round your mouth?" The boy wiped it quickly.

"Nothin'," he said.

"It was meal, wasn't it?" said Captain Watt.

"We was give it," said John, "we're awful hungry most o' the time."

"An' I don't feel well either, Sir" added Jimmy.

"Who gave ye the meal?"

"I canna say," said John.

The Captain slapped John around the face.

"Don't go beggin' off the crew, I won't have it."

"It's not fair…" began Jimmy. "We…" He was stopped by a cuff around the head. Now both boys were close to tears.

"I say what's fair or not," said the Captain. "As I said tae the Irishman, if you're not happy wi' what ye's bein' fed, ye can always leave the ship."

"I'd leave now if I had somewhere else tae go," Jimmy murmured, as the Captain dissolved into the mist, "if that ice was land, I'd be gone now."

"Me too," said John, rubbing a reddened cheek. "Long ago."

By four o' clock the mist had lifted and the sun had broken through to spangle the ice with light. It was at times so bright that it was difficult to look at. Here and there, seals broke the still whiteness, appearing suddenly and disappearing just as quickly. The coast of Newfoundland, although distant, was bluish, but crystal clear. It was all the more frustrating to the stowaways that land was tantalisingly only just out of reach.

The Captain had again been busy, looking at the land from the poop and had climbed to the masthead to scan the horizon with his telescope. After being aloft for half an hour, he returned to the deck. He called to the Mate and then went down into the saloon. He was Joined By Kerr, whose breath stank of whisky.

Kerr held his pipe up in front of him. "Mind if I smoke?"

"No, carry on, I'll join ye." Watt took his pipe from a drawer and began to fill it with tobacco as the Mate lit up. He too lit his pipe and drew several mouthfuls of smoke to get it going. Satisfied that all was well he opened a thick blue cloth-covered book and thumbed through it.

"Ah, yes, the Myrtle," he murmured, and then looked up. "There's a barque close tae the shore. If I've read the flags right she's the Myrtle."

"Oh yes, I know her," said Kerr. "Left Greenock a week or so before us. What of her?"

"If I send the stowboys ashore, she could be a halfway house for them."

"Ye still want rid o'em?"

"Aye, the sooner the better – the ice looks good."

"But not the little ones?"

"Aye, them too, get rid o' the lot – lock, stock and barrel."

They smoked for a few minutes in silence, the clouds of smoke mingling and climbing into the lantern light in the saloon. The Captain was the first to break the silence.

"I'd like tae go down on the ice and check it out. I need tae look around the hull anyway. Gi' it ten minutes an' we'll get Hunter and Hendry down on the ice. Get 'em tae bring a couple o' boat hooks an' a large axe. I don't like the way the ice is encroachin' on the hull. We may need tae clear it."

Brand was scraping the poop deck when he saw the little group of men descend to the ice. The four men walked a few hundred yards out from the ship, making their way across the white expanse without much difficulty, skirting the piled ice and turquoise ponds. The Captain and Mate were talking and pointing in various directions.

Brand knew that they would be on the ice for some time and so decided to look for something to eat. Most of the crew were forward, some of them watching the group of figures on the ice. He casually strolled to the rail of the poop and, after a further glance around, quickly went into the stern quarters.

The aroma of pipe tobacco was strong as he tiptoed to the pantry. Opening the door carefully, he found some broken biscuits on a plate. He ate these while he searched for further food. In a small meat safe he found another plate, upon which were some slices of beef and more broken biscuit. Although the sortie had lasted little more than a minute or two, he became anxious that he might get caught if he remained much longer. Stuffing what he couldn't immediately eat into his pockets, he made his way to the deck, checking that no-one was around before emerging on to the deck. He polished a brass embellishment on leaving, to help dispel any suspicions, should anyone be watching.

But he was seen, by Bryson, who had been scraping the deck of the poop, but further back, by the ship's wheel. He sat back on his haunches. Brand smiled at him and raised his eyebrows. He was chewing. Without speaking he took up his scraper and continued his task.

Bryson too, began scraping again. His hands were cold and sore from the work and he was so hungry. He cast a glance over to Brand, who appeared to be feeding himself from his pocket. Finally, Bryson stood up, stretching his cold stiffened legs. He went to the rail and, to his amazement couldn't see anyone on the ice. 'Where are they?' he thought. A sudden movement at the corner of his eye solved the mystery. They were on the ice at the bows of the Arran, busy with fenders and ropes.

After a cursory look around, he went down into the stern quarters.

Kerr had been working with a boat hook, trying to break the ice away from the bow of the ship.

"Oh, this is no good. The ice is too thick. Gimme the fellin' axe will ye'."

"Fellin' axe?" queried Hendry.

"Aye, fellin' axe," repeated Kerr with exasperation.

"We havena' brought an axe down."

"Don't ye listen? I told ye tae bring one."

"Sorry Sir, I didna hear ye say that. I'll go an' get it now."

"No, I'll get it," said Kerr, "I have tae do somethin else, so I can kill two birds wi' one stone."

The thing that he had to do was to refill his hip flask. He had found the walk across the ice colder than he had expected and had taken several 'nips' to warm himself. He was surprised at how quickly the flask ran dry.

Kerr walked along the ice to the ladder and climbed to the deck. As his head appeared over the rail his eye was drawn to a flash of light reflected from the stern quarters companionway door as it was opened. A head cautiously peered out.

It wasn't until the Mate was running across the deck towards him that Bryson noticed him. His mouth dropped open in horrified surprise. Before he could run, Kerr was upon him, cuffing him around the head and swearing. He grabbed the youth and shook him roughly.

"What ye doin' in officers' quarters – heh?"

All Bryson could do was to let out a defensive torrent of pleas of innocence.

"I was only following Brand," said Bryson. "I didn't steal nothin', honest."

The raised voices brought the steward McLean out of the galley. Kerr spotted him.

"McLean. Get Brand and bring him here." He drew a thin line of cord from his pocket and tied Bryson's hands. Brand was brought from the poop to the main deck to join Bryson, who was still struggling.

"Search their pockets will ye," ordered Kerr.

The steward searched through Brand's pockets and found nothing, but when he went through Bryson's he found a handful of currants, which he showed to the Mate.

"Ah, ye thievin' bastard!" he said, "Ye'll pay dearly for those." Kerr tripped and pushed Bryson to the deck. "Put the currants back into his pocket," he ordered.

While this was being done, Kerr tied Bryson's hands to a ring-bolt in the deck. The youth was crying and pleading mournfully.

The Mate strode off to the Arran's bow and called down to the Captain on the ice. To Bryson's dismay, he returned quickly with a fiery look of determination on his face. He released him from his bonds.

"Get undressed," he ordered.

"Oh no, please Sir, oh please!" He adopted a praying attitude and dropped on to his knees, tears falling from his chin.

"Please sir, I was starvin'. Oh please sir don't beat me, I was so hungry."

"Get up," ordered the Mate. The youth complied, but was now sobbing loudly.

"Get undressed and stop that bloody whinin'."

Bryson fumbled with the buttons of his coat. When they were all undone Kerr pulled roughly on the coat to remove it.

"Come on boy, hurry up."

With the assistance of the Mate and Steward Bryson stripped completely naked. He shivered uncontrollably and again put his hands together in supplication. Kerr used this action to once more tie his hands. Bryson went down on to his knees swearing before God that he would never steal again. Raising a heavy boot the Mate kicked him over on to his side and then, with McLean holding his legs, tied his feet together.

Kerr sneered at the youth and sauntered casually over to the pin rail. He took a bundle of rope from one of the pins, found the end and dropped the remainder on the deck. As he slowly returned to the youth he thumbed a knot into the end of the rope.

Bryson had no doubt as to what came next and his cries for clemency became louder and higher in pitch, almost screaming. Kerr was smiling, but his eyes were on fire.

The sound of the youth's cries echoed out over the ice and drew an audience. Many of the off duty watch had come up from below and some climbed into the lower part of the shrouds to gain a better view.

As Kerr ran the rope through his hand Bryson closed his eyes and braced himself for the assault. He screamed and arched his back as the rope bit home.

"Please, please!" he sobbed. After six lashes the beating stopped. Bryson still had his eyes closed. He was surprised when his ankles were grasped and his legs were pulled skywards. He opened his eyes and saw that the Captain had returned and had taken up the rope. Kerr was pulling on his legs and adjusted his grip to behind the youth's knees. He was now upside down with his head clear of the ground and was looking between the Mate's legs.

He began pleading again but his soft pleas turned into screams as the lashing re-commenced. After ten or more strokes of the rope he began to choke on his mucus and was then allowed to drop to the deck.

Through the distortion of his tears he saw the Captain striding off and thought that his ordeal was over. He began to rise but a hard kick in the ribs from Kerr sent him sprawling.

"Get on your knees," Kerr's voice was coldly boiling.

Bryson, gasping for air, complied.

The Mate then launched on a seemingly endless torrent of blows across the youth's back. The crew members and stowaways watched in horrified silence as mark after livid mark crossed Bryson's back and legs. Only occasionally did the youth flinch and the violent screams that at first tore out over the cold white expanse, gave way to gasps and moans. Three times he tried to rise but was kicked to the deck.

When the Mate had spent his fury, he stood back and, still holding the rope, told Niven, the second Mate, to untie Bryson, who was face down on the deck and groaning.

"Get up!" Kerr's voice was hoarse.

Bryson started to rise but found that the swollen weals restricted his movement. Not only were they painful, they actually felt tight, like rope bonds.

" McLean," said Kerr. "Cut all the pockets out o' his coat an' get a plate an' put the currants on it. The wee stowboys can share them."

The plate was put upon the hatch cover and the four boys fought for their share. Bryson, still totally naked, stood with his head hung. He was quaking from head to foot and a string of thick saliva ran from his mouth and hung from his chin. His eyes were red, their lids swollen and purple veined. They did not appear focused.

Kerr snatched a broom from one of the deckhands and thrust it towards the youth.

"Ye can sweep the poop deck now. Tidy up all the scrapings." He turned to the audience that remained. "Alright, the entertainment's over, ye can return tae ye's work."

They dispersed, muttering among themselves.

Bryson worked almost mechanically, moving stiffly and drawing breath in hisses, through clenched teeth. More than once his legs weakened and he had to lean on the broom for support.

Kerr, meanwhile, had taken the two shirts that Bryson had worn and given one each to Hughie and Jimmy.

## 24. *Sent ashore*

After half an hour of sweeping Bryson was allowed to put on his vest and trousers. For a while, he sat down on the main hatch cover. Kerr sauntered cockily over to him, took the thin line, which had tied his hands during the beating, from his pocket, folded it neatly into four and gently struck the palm of his open hand with it, clasping it and pulling it from the loose grip. He repeated this movement several times before speaking to the youth.

"We found tobacco in your pockets, besides the currants. Where did ye get it?"

"I was give it by one o' the sailors."

"Liar!" Kerr struck the youth sharply across the shoulder with the line.

"I'll say anything ye want me tae say, Sir, only please don't beat me any more." he began to cry.

"I was honestly give it by Angus Clark – ask him. I've already bin punished for the tobacco I stole. Please Sir, it's the truth." He wiped his eyes with the backs of his hands. He was trembling.

Kerr looked at him and smiled with satisfaction.

"Ye can go tae the deck house now."

Bryson painfully stood up and walked to the deck house. He opened the door to go into the sail room.

"Bryson!" Kerr's voice was sharp and made the youth jump. He looked back. The Mate's tone softened. "On top, boy, not inside."

Feeling pain in every movement, he climbed to the roof of the deck house and leaned carefully against one of the boats.

"Tha's better," said Kerr.

At eight o' clock the following morning, the stowaways assembled in the sail room for their meagre breakfast of a mug of coffee and three small pieces of biscuit. They had been at work since being woken at four. They all sat, wrapped as warmly as they could be, with their hands clamped around their mugs.

Through the open door of the room they could see Captain Watt on the poop, busy with telescope and a chart, which occasional gusts of wind tried to tear from his hands. Earlier he had been aloft and had spent a fair while looking towards the land.

"Look at him," said Brand. "Somethin's up – he's hardly taken his eyes off land since sun up."

"Oi t'ink he's goin' to send us ashore across de oice," said Reilly.

"I hope he does," said Bryson.

"I don't," answered Brand.

"Nor do I," added John.

Brand raised his hands in emphasis. "It doesna look safe tae me. We're better off where we are."

"Some o' ye may be," said Bryson, casting an accusatory glance at Currie.

"If de oice is alright, I'll go," said Reilly.

"Trouble is, it might be alright for a few miles, but what if it…"

Brand's words cut off as the Captain called for Reilly. The Irishman placed his bowler on his head, patted its top and walked to the poop.

"It's got tae be about goin' ashore," said Brand.

As Reilly approached the Captain he was given the telescope and the officer pointed to various places, which Reilly tried to follow with the instrument. Captain Watt finally took the telescope back and after a minute or two of further discussion, during which the Captain glanced and motioned towards the sailroom, he returned to his colleagues.

"He wants us tae walk ashore doesn't he?" said Brand.

Reilly paused before replying.

"Yes…" he began. "He said he could see houses on shore, but when I looked it was still too far to see anythin' clearly. I'm for goin' if there are houses. There could have been houses – a bit too far to see."

"Watt says there are houses doesn't he?" said Bryson.

"Aye, but he says it was clearer yesterday – easier to make things out."

"He wouldn't lie about that would he?"

"I wouldn't think so."

"If you're willin' tae go I'll come wi' ye. I've had enough o' it."

"So we'll go shall we?"

"Aye."

Brand stamped his mug down on to a shelf. "What ye do is up tae you, but I'm not goin' – how d'ye know the ice goes tae shore? – ye don't."

"The Captain has been aloft God knows how many times. He wouldn't send us unless it was safe."

"Well, I don't fancy the idea, I got no shoes," said John.

"Neither have I," said Jimmy, "an' I got a chill."

"You look alright tae me," said Bryson.

Jimmy responded quickly, "I cut my foot last time I was on the ice."

"I don't want tae go either," said Hughie.

"Well, there's a surprise," said Bryson with light sarcasm, "and I suppose our little bum boy Currie won't want tae leave his friends."

"You leave me alone," said Currie, "I'm not a bum boy an' I don't want tae go either."

"Bloody feeble objects, the lot o'ye," said Bryson. He turned to Reilly. "Come on Barney, let's get our stuff together."

"No offence lads," said Reilly, "but I'll take my chance wid de oice."

They left the cabin and walked towards the poop, where the Captain was waiting.

"Idiots!" muttered Brand.

"I'm not goin'," said John.

"Nor am I," added Jimmy.

Their breakfast over, the stowaways wrapped themselves as well as they could and went about their duties. John went down into the crew quarters in the forecastle, where a seaman was showing him how to make mats from disused rope. The sailor explained that the mats were used to protect the sides of the ship when loading or unloading cargo.

Hughie and Jimmy were scraping the deck of the forecastle head, while Brand coiled ropes near the poop rail. Currie was tidying in one of the holds. Bryson, whose coat now had no pockets, made a small bundle of his belongings, tied it together with string and hung it around his neck. He had found a long stick in the hold and thought that it may be useful on the ice and so took it with him. When they returned to the deck the Captain was waiting by the ladder.

"Follow me," he said, descending to the ice.

Bryson dropped his stick on to the ice and climbed down, closely followed by Reilly. The Captain, for a change, seemed almost jovial.

"Right lads, if you take the route straight ahead ye'll get ashore alright. There's a ship called the Myrtle in the ice a little offshore – ye can get some victuals from her if ye have the need. Just aim for that headland there." He pointed. "There's a break in the cliffs wi' a wee beach. That'll lead ye tae the houses."

"The oice does go tae the shore?" asked Reilly.

"It looks solid tae the shore from the masthead," said Watt.

"Ah well, we'll be off then Sir," said Reilly, offering his hand.

The Captain ignored the gesture. "Wait a few minutes will ye? I'll see if any o'the others want tae come wi' ye."

On climbing back on board he saw Currie and told him to tell the other stowaways that they were wanted on deck. In the meantime, he went to the galley and returned with his pockets filled with biscuits.

"Right my fine lads…" he began. The boys looked at one another, amazed at the uncharacteristic joviality. "Mister Reilly and Master Bryson are walking ashore. Those who want tae go wi' 'em get a biscuit; those who don't, don't. Now, who wants to go ashore?" He held up a biscuit in each hand and smiled as if it was a game.

"I'd like a biscuit, please Sir," said Jimmy. He stepped forward and took one from the Captain's hand.

"That's the way – come on lads," said the officer. All but Brand took a biscuit and began to eagerly gnaw them.

"Right ye are lads, get ye's things together. Mr Reilly and Master Bryson won't want tae be kept waitin'."

Several minutes went by and no-one reappeared on deck. The Captain by now was becoming irritated. He noticed Brand coiling ropes and went up to him. "Are ye goin' ashore?" he asked, with as pleasant a manner as his irritability would allow.

"No Sir, I didn't take a biscuit. I'll bide 'til we reach Quebec."

The veneer of civility peeled away. "Oh no ye won't. If I need to, I'll make ye go."

"Well Sir, with respect, I won't go unless I'm made to. I don't think it's safe."

Captain Watt flung out his arm and pointed to the bows. "Get up tae the fo'c's'le now!"

Brand didn't move.

"Sir, I…"

"Move or ye'll get a rope's end!"

Somewhat stunned, the youth did as he was told. As he walked across the deck he saw Reilly and Bryson waiting, some fifty yards from the ship. They looked so small and insignificant against the vast white panorama. Land was but a vague blue/grey smudge on the horizon. Brand, with reluctance, climbed into the fore rigging, but was determined to stay there unless forced down. The Captain's attention turned to the other stowaways who then arrived. He took Hughie's arm first.

"Right, over ye go."

The boy pulled against the Captain's grip and began to cry.

"Please don't make me go. I don't want tae go. Please Sir, please!"

The Captain swung the boy up and sat him on the rail.

"Ye can either go down o'ye's own accord, or I'll throw ye down!"

Hughie took the rope and hand over hand let himself down to the ice.

Jimmy too, was crying.

"I can't go down on the ice, Sir, not wi' no shoes. It's too long a way wi' no shoes. I'll die for sure."

"Well, ye might as well die on the ice as on board this ship, 'cause ye'll get nae more food from me."

He lifted the boy on to the rail and motioned for him to descend.

"Can I have somethin' tae put on my feet, Sir?"

"Just get down boy! Do as ye's told."

Still sobbing, Jimmy went down.

Currie was next in line. His eyes were full of tears. The Captain put his hand on the boy's shoulder. As he did so John, who had hung back, quietly took some backward steps, eventually turning and creeping down the forecastle companionway into the crew quarters. He opened one of the larger of the seamen's trunks, pulled out the clothing within, and threw it under a bunk. He then climbed in. He could hear the Captain calling for him as he closed down the lid. In the close confines of the trunk his breathing and heartbeat to him sounded loud enough to wake the dead.

He heard a noise. Was it someone coming into the cabin? It went quiet. He held his breath. Only the boom, boom of his heart broke the silence. He opened the trunk lid a little. It creaked. Through the crack he saw Currie, and Currie, still crying, saw him.

"Don't tell on me, Peter, please don't tell." A noise made John put the lid back down, but barely a second later it was thrown back; he was lifted out by the ears. The Captain frogmarched the boy up to the deck. He was struggling to get away and was almost hysterical. Seeing the Mate walking on the poop, he managed to pull away and ran to him. He dropped on to his knees and begged not to be sent ashore.

"I'll have nothing tae do wi' sendin ye ashore," said Kerr grimly.

John clutched at the Mate's legs but was dragged away by the Captain. The boy struggled all the way to where the others had gone over the side and, as he had done with the other boys, the Captain swung John up on to the rail.

"Hold the rope, damn ye," said the Captain. John held the rope with one hand and clung like a limpet to the rail with the other.

"Let go!" said Watt, but rather than letting go, he was trying to climb back. The Captain took a belaying pin from the pin-rail nearby and struck the boy hard on the shoulder. John half slid and half fell onto the ice, landing on his side. For a moment he was winded. Brand helped him to his feet and the little group made their way to the stern from where Kerr was watching.

"Can we have some food for the walk? It's an awful long way," said Brand.

"Ye can have one biscuit each," said Kerr. "Wait there."

A biscuit was thrown to each of the waiting boys. The one thrown to John was poorly aimed and just touched the tips of his fingers, then smashed to a dozen fragments on the ice.

## 25. *The long walk*

Hughie, half sliding on the slippery ice, helped his friend to his feet. John was still crying and holding his side.

"Come on Johnny." He put his arm around his shoulder, "We'll be alright. We'll stick together, yes?"

John nodded and they hurried after the others who were walking purposefully away from the ship. Reilly and Bryson led, Brand and Jimmy walked together, a little behind them.

John was surprised at how much firmer the ice had become since he had gone down for the peelings. But it was still uneven and sprinkled with gritty patches, but the frosting of snow had melted away in the bright sun.

They had been walking for ten minutes when Hughie heard the faint sound of shouting behind them. They stopped and looked back to the Arran. Many of the crew were looking in their direction. John thought that he could see the Captain and Mate standing together at the stern. The one he believed to be the Mate cupped his hands around his mouth and shouted something. The words were lost in the distance between them. Hughie thought it odd that he took his hands away from his mouth and waved before the sound of his voice stopped.

"I wonder what that was about," he said, waving back.

"Makin' fun o' us I expect," said John.

"D'ye think they heard ye?" asked the Captain, a note of concern in his voice.

"The telegraph boy waved, so I suppose he heard," said Kerr.

"The bigger ones are still stridin' out. They didn't hear."

"Well, if they get into difficulties they'll be back, whether they heard or not," said Kerr. "If they get hungry they'll be back for their dinner."

They continued watching the stowaways' slow, slippery progress across the white expanse in silence. The older ones began to pull away from the younger boys. Hughie had fallen twice and was being helped along by John and McGinnes.

When the little group were about a half mile away the Captain began to see the minute figures' crawling pace in relation to the distance that had to be traversed. Another boy fell and was helped to his feet. He seemed to be limping. The Captain turned to Kerr, who shrugged – as if to say that it was nothing to do with him – and then turned to walk off. The Captain put his hand on the Mate's arm.

"D'ye think we should send someone to fetch 'em back?"

Kerr thought for a second and looked at the distant figures.

"No, I'll wager they'll all be back for their dinner."

The ice was not flat and in places where the pans had been driven one on top of the other, they were up to seven feet high. As the figures wove their way around these, they were lost to view from the ship. Each time the Captain watched anxiously until they reappeared.

As the sun climbed higher into the sky the glare off the ice became almost painful and he found it difficult to keep them under constant observation. Finally the intervening obstacles so masked the stowaways that they could only occasionally be seen. Each time Watt counted them. "One, two, three, four, five, six."

When he had not seen them for more than five minutes he became agitated and after a while of pacing about the deck, climbed to the main crosstree, viewing their progress through his telescope.

"Wait for us!" called John to the older lads, who were by now a hundred yards or so ahead of them. The youths stopped and beckoned their frustration at having to wait.

Bryson looked back at the ship. Increasingly he found the brightness of the ice hard to cope with and his eyes were squinting. The Arran was hardly visible now. Only the upper masts could be seen.

John, Jimmy and Hughie joined the others.

"For God's sake keep up," said Brand irritably. "We've got tae make shore before sunset or we're done for. At this rate we'll still be on the ice 'til Christmas."

"It would be nice if we knew that we were goin' in the right direction," added Bryson.

"The Captain explained the way tae go quite clearly," said Reilly curtly. "We're goin' the right way so far. We should see the Myrtle soon."

"Are ye sure?" asked Brand.

"Ye bloody better be," said Bryson.

"I'm sure," said Reilly irritably. Jimmy began to limp and was crying.

"Wha's the matter now?" said Bryson.

"I've hurt me foot," sobbed the boy. He sat against an ice boulder and rubbed the white, waxy-looking foot.

"Oh, for Christ's sake!" gasped Bryson, "why are we saddled wi' these babies?"

"It's alright for you," said John, "We've nae shoes. It's murder walkin."

"Come on Jimmy, there's a good lad – keep goin'," said Brand, wearily.

"I've just realised," said John, "Where's Peter Currie?"

"Ye mean ye's actually surprised he wasna put on the ice wi' us?" said Bryson, "I'd have been surprised if he had been."

For a distance of about three miles the ice was reasonably sound and level with only occasional humps and hollows. The sun began to give some warmth and they made good progress. At one point Bryson and Reilly were singing, their voices lost into the emptiness.

Hughie began to feel weary. He kept falling behind and had to keep trotting to catch up. The ice's surface was glistening as it began to melt. Pans which had previously been frozen together to make a continuous surface, began to move independently, grating against one another in the currents and leaving black water between them here and there.

The pace slowed considerably. In some places the joins between the pans could be stepped over, in others it was necessary to jump from one to the other across the water. Crushed ice that looked like a frothy scum bobbed on the water between the floes.

"This isn't too clever," said Brand, reaching out for Bryson's hand as he jumped from one pan to another. The stride was misjudged and he landed on the broken edge of the floe. This gave way and a gout of water was thrown up as he went in up to his waist. Bryson gasped with the cold shock of the water. He might have gone under but his stick cracked down on to the firm ice to either side and prevented him from sinking further. Brand quickly grabbed him and pulled him on to firmer ice.

"Christ, you nearly had me in too," said Brand. Streaming water he stood up, still trying to catch his breath. He began to shiver.

It was while crossing on to the very next pan that both Brand and Reilly fell into the water. Reilly had already crossed and was waiting, his arm outstretched, to take Brand's hand. He hesitated on the edge.

"It's a bit far tae step. I'll jump across." He took a few steps back and leaped across the crumbled join. He landed well on to the firm ice but the sudden shock of his weight caused it to crack. The portion on which he and Reilly were standing tipped and they both slid into the water. Their waterlogged clothes and the slipperiness of the ice made getting out difficult. With great effort and the help of the others they clawed their way back on to the firm ice to stand, drenched and shivering, while trying to gasp away the shock of the cold upon their bodies.

Reilly had lost his hat. He could see it floating brim-uppermost among the scummy melting ice. Kneeling carefully, he reached out but couldn't reach it. Bryson offered him his stick, but Reilly only managed to push it under the ice.

"Bloody nuisance," he said, "A fine hat was that. Cost me a shillin'."

Brand wiped the water from his face. "Look, this is crazy. See that, over there?" He pointed to a black line to his left and followed it as it crossed their path a few hundred yards ahead.

"That's a lane o' water. I bet it goes on for miles. We can't cross that." The others looked. Brand continued, "And look how broken the ice is getting'." He looked to his right. The ice seemed better. "I think we should change direction – head over this way, straight for that headland." He pointed to the grey shadow in the distance.

"But tha's a cliff," protested Reilly, "How can we climb that?"

"There's probably a way up."

"We were told to go this way," said Reilly. "The Captain said…"

"I don't care what the bloody Captain said," interrupted Brand. "Look how far we have tae go." He pointed to the still distant land. "We've been walkin' for ages an' it doesnae look any closer. An' what do we do when we get tae that strip o' water?"

"It might be better further on," reasoned Reilly. "Perhaps we can get around the water."

Brand became irritable. "I'm goin this way. If ye want tae carry on the way ye's goin' then please y'sels." He walked away from the group.

"I'm wi' Davie Brand," said Jimmy, following him.

John and Hughie looked from Brand to Reilly, who in turn was judging the options. 'The way ahead is a lot more broken, and there's that lane of water – it must be at least thirty feet wide. It's true that the ice looks better in the direction that Brand has taken – but for how long?' He thought

"Well, which way are ye goin' tae go?" asked Bryson. Reilly looked again at the ice ahead.

"Oh, we'll try his way," he said. The group followed on.

Frustrated by having to continually wait for the little ones, and in particular Hughie, who was finding it very difficult, and conscious of how far they had to go, Reilly made a proposition.

"Look," he said quietly to Brand. "We need to move faster than this. What if we go on ahead, leave Bryson and the little ones to go at their own pace. When we make land we can get help. If we don't get a shift on we're all goin' to die."

Bryson overheard.

"I think we should all stick together."

"I think that Barney's right," said Brand. "We have tae get a move on. I mean we must have been walkin for four hours an' we're still in the middle o' nowhere. We have tae go on at our own pace." He looked at the astonished faces of the smaller boys and immediately felt guilty.

"If ye can keep up wi us, that's fine. If ye can't, I promise we'll be back for ye as soon as we can get help."

"Don't leave us," pleaded Hughie, bursting into tears.

The older ones shut their ears to his appeal and strode off. Bryson looked back to see Hughie fall over yet again, to be helped to his feet by John. This made up his mind and he hurried after the older ones.

Jimmy, seeing the gap between himself and the three widening, struggled to increase his pace, but his feet felt as if they were made of wood; there was no feeling in them and he kept stumbling. But even at his pace he was widening the gap between himself and John and Hughie.

"They're leavin' us behind," wailed Hughie.

"We've got tae go faster," urged John. "Come on now, for God's sake try tae go a bit faster." He began to cry and tried to pull his friend along. "Come on… we got to step out."

The older boys were making good progress at first and when he looked back Brand could only see Jimmy – a small figure in the distance, but before long the ice again became more broken and uneven. In some parts the action of sun, wind and water had sculpted the ice into small hills, valleys and lakes. There were potholes and areas of swelling black water between the pans. Each of the floes moved independently to the rhythm of the tide. The pathfinders fought to find a way through, and the stragglers caught up with them. John slipped and fell into a shallow pond that had formed in a depression in the ice. He pulled Hughie over as he fell. He was soaked through and had difficulty clambering up the sloping sides.

Everyone was becoming tired. Those who hadn't themselves fallen in had become soaked in the struggle to help the others out. They were also hungry. Hazy cloud dimmed the heat of the sun and yet did not reduce the glare from the surface of the ice. Both Hughie and Bryson were finding the blinding light difficult. Hughie was sneezing and blinking away tears. Bryson too had to keep wiping his eyes, which were now becoming sore. He also found that he could no longer feel either of his feet. Both John's and Jimmy's bare feet were now blue and were becoming swollen. They had long since lost any feeling.

"Ye've hurt youse foot," said Reilly to John.

"Have I?" said the boy looking down to see a red stain appear with every step of his right foot. John stood on one leg and looked at the sole of his foot. There was a cut on the underside of a middle toe. It oozed sluggishly.

"Didn't know I'd done that," he said lightly, but knowing it was there, he began to limp.

The older boys had felt bad about leaving the little ones behind and were glad that circumstances had allowed them to catch up. None now suggested leaving the slower boys.

Brand thought it best that they should not move across the ice as a group, but should walk in single file with six yards between each person. This would mean that less weight would be imposed on the ice, but rescue would be at hand should anyone be in difficulties.

Jimmy was the next to fall in the water. He misjudged a jump and the edge of the pan gave way and he went down. Bryson offered the end of his stick, which he quickly grasped and was dragged out. Even before this immersion, Jimmy, without shoes and in holed threadbare clothes, was shivering. He now wrapped his arms around himself to try to reduce the violent quaking that gripped him. He was sobbing.

Hughie was again trailing behind. He stumbled constantly; the hobnails causing him to skid on the ice, and often he had to flail his arms to regain his balance, sometimes unsuccessfully. He was very pale and shivered consistently. John hurried up to Bryson to ask him to help Hughie to cross from one pan to another. Before Bryson could offer his stick to the boy, Hughie slipped and fell into the water. He was quickly pulled out by Bryson but was choking on water he had inhaled. His cap was gone.

'It's strange,' thought Bryson, 'I don't think I've ever seen him without that great big cap on. How small his head looks without it.' Hughie coughed until red spots of blood stained the ice. He was helped to his feet but his knees gave way as he had a second bout of coughing.

"I'll be all right in a minute," he gasped, "Wait for me won't you?"

Bryson was hurrying after the others who were now about a hundred yards ahead. John grabbed his friend's arm and they staggered on together. There was a slight downward slope on the next pan and as they reached the edge John jumped the two feet and turned to be soaked by a gout of water as Hughie again fell in the water. Before John could lend a hand he had managed to pull himself out and for a few seconds he lay spluttering on the ice. John helped him to his feet, looking at the figures ahead becoming smaller by the minute. He cupped his hands and shouted "Wait for us. Please wait!"

## 26. *The ice claims its victims*

"We've got tae catch up, Hughie," John looked anxiously at the distant figures. "Come on, Hurry up."

Hughie caught his breath and began a bout of coughing which stopped him in his tracks.

John cried tears of frustration. "Wait for us!" he screamed. No one turned or slowed their pace. Unconsciously, he had walked a little way ahead of his friend.

"Don't leave me," pleaded Hughie.

John looked back, surprised at the ten yards that were between them. He waited for his friend to join him and they carried on as best they could.

At the edge of the next pan there were a number of smaller pieces, which were moving and grating against one another.

"We canna clear these wi' a jump" said John. "We'll have tae try doin' steppin' stones. If I hold your hand you step on to that big piece there. I'll follow an' then we'll cross tae the other pan over there." He pointed.

Holding hands, Hughie tentatively stepped from the edge of the floe, across two feet of gently surging black water, on to the moving edge of the smaller pan. Before he could transfer his weight he slipped and both boys found themselves in the water. For a second Hughie disappeared but then rose, choking and kicking. John was gasping for air, thrashing about and scrabbling at the edge of a pan. He felt Hughie grab his jacket and was pulled under. Kicking even harder he freed himself and rose to the surface. Clawing at the slippery edge of the ice, he eventually found a grip and pulled himself out. He turned to help his friend but was horrified to see that the two pans were converging. Hughie was fighting hard to stay on the surface, but the weight of his boots and clothes were too great. Again he went under and John saw the top of his head disappear from sight as the ice pans closed up and grated together over him.

"Hughie!" he screamed, "Hughie!"

There was no gap now. John stood, horrified and unbelieving. He let out an ear piercing scream and stared at the edges of the ice, willing them to open.

Upon hearing the scream first Brand, then Bryson, ran back to see what had happened. Bryson tried to use his stick to prise the pans apart but it just slipped as small pieces crumbled away. There was nothing more that could be done. They waited for two minutes, then Brand put his arm around John's shoulder and led him away.

"Come on Johnny. If it helps, I don't think he'd have made it anyway."

John walked mechanically, stunned by Hughie's death. He kept up with the bigger boys and scarcely noticed the passage of time. He was also unaware that Jimmy was beginning to fall behind, only catching up when the group was traversing difficult areas, or when they waited for him. He was irritable, grumbling about the pace and how no-one was waiting for him.

The sun had passed its zenith and was falling steadily into the afternoon sky. They had been on the ice for seven hours. Bryson was now walking with difficulty, stumbling and falling regularly. His eyelids were becoming swollen and the whites of his eyes were bloodshot. His cheeks were continually wet with the tears that flowed. The warming effect of the sun was waning, to be replaced by a gusting wind that chilled the lads to the marrow. Their clothes were stiff with the cold. Reilly was the only one who seemed largely unaffected by the ordeal they had suffered.

Jimmy was in a poor state: shivering violently, his feet and ankles grossly swollen and blotchily blue. He walked as if drunk, and found difficulty in responding, when spoken to. When he did speak, it was to complain.

A lone cloud obscured the hazy light of the sun, sending an extra chill through their bodies. The ice was good at this point. For the past few miles it had been fairly level and they were able to make good time, despite having to stop now and again to allow Jimmy to catch up.

"Hold on Davie," said Reilly. "He's way behind again." They watched as the boy staggered blindly towards them. They could hear him panting with effort, his breath in great clouds. "He's not goin' to make it," he whispered, shaking his head.

Reilly looked at the headland and the distance that still had to be traversed. He could see vegetation staining the hard rock of the cliffs and the sea breaking on rocks at their foot. He could even see seabirds perching and wheeling around them. There were buildings on the cliff top, silhouetted against the blue of the sky.

"How many miles now, d'ye reckon?" asked Reilly.

"Dunno. Maybe three or four. I'm not much good wi' distances," answered Brand, shivering.

Reilly looked up at the sun. "We should make land before sunset, God willing."

Reilly looked back to Jimmy, who after staggering sideways for a yard or so fell on the ice. He was groaning and seemed to find it difficult to get up. As Brand went back to help him he struggled to his feet, tottered to a lump of ice and wearily sat down on it. He was muttering as Brand approached.

"Oh, Ma, I'm so weary. So weary. I wish I could awa' tae me bed." His ears, nose, lips and chin were quite blue and his eyelids had swollen considerably. His fingers were curled into fists and were quite a dark, greyish blue. It was odd that, unlike the others, his violent shivering had stopped. He saw Brand and spoke wearily.

"Ah, Davie. Have ye come tae get me? I canna go on any farther on my own. Ye won't leave me will ye?"

Reilly came up.

"He says he can't go on any further," explained Brand.

"Jimmy, ye've got to go on. If ye stay here ye'll die," said Reilly.

"Come on laddie! Not much further – just a bit more effort," Brand pleaded.

"No, I canna go no further. Look at ma poor feet. Can ye carry me?"

"We can't carry ye. It's hard enough makin' for ourselves," said Reilly. Brand pulled Jimmy's arm away from his body with difficulty, put his head underneath it and tried to lift the boy to his feet. Jimmy's legs would not support him at all. Brand allowed him to sit back on the lump of ice.

"It's hopeless. I wouldn't last five minutes carryin' him along."

"Well…" said Reilly, pausing, unhappy with what he had to say next, "I'm afraid we're goin' to have to leave him."

Brand bit his lip. "Yes, I suppose we are."

"No, don't leave me please!" Jimmy pleaded, tears filling his eyes.

"We canna carry ye. It would finish us all," said Brand.

"We'll send help as soon as we make land, that's a promise."

"It's for the best," added Reilly.

John looked back and watched as Reilly and Brand walked away from the little boy. Both were crying. As the four walked on, Jimmy's desperate cries tore sharply through the brittle air and into their consciences.

"Please take me wi' ye… Help me *please*… help me, oh, sweet Jesus, please help me… Oh, Ma, where are ye?"

Gradually the sound of his voice faded. When it could no longer be heard John turned and looked back. In the distance, a tiny dark figure against the vast white plain still sat where they had left him.

John was surprised to see that with every footstep he had left a red stain on the ice. Both feet were now bleeding. They didn't hurt – he had had no feeling in them since shortly after leaving the Arran – but they felt odd, as if he were walking on sponges.

Looking ahead, the group walked on. The quality of the ice varied between good and atrocious. When it was good they strode out and where it was broken progress was difficult and slow. Brand and Reilly began to pull away from Bryson and John, and it was only because the leaders stopped now and again that they caught up. Three hours had passed since they had left Jimmy and the sun was on its descent to the horizon. The wind had changed and was coming from the land. Tantalisingly, they could smell woodsmoke.

The ice now became very broken and sculptured. Finding a way through was extremely slow work and they all slipped and fell into pools of icy water and into the sea. Bryson's eyes were now so swollen that he could hardly see. He complained that they felt as if grit had got into them. Brand had to lead him by the hand.

John was still picturing Hughie's last few moments in his mind. He saw it over and over again. His own scream of terror tore repeatedly through him, echoing into the infinity of the ice. His shivering, although still violent, now came in phases. He was pleased when it stopped. It was such an effort. Sometimes it seemed that he was an onlooker and his mind drifted so that he felt that he wasn't on the ice at all. He became irritated when Brand tried to help him across a difficult, broken area.

"I can manage, I'm not a bairn," he said.

Reilly noticed a black line between the foamed rocks at the foot of the cliffs and the edge of the ice. As they fought, foot by foot and pan by pan towards the cliffs, it became clear that there was a considerably wide lane of water between the edge of the ice field and the land.

"I don't believe it," said Brand. "I thought that bastard of a Captain told ye that the ice went tae the land?"

"He did."

"Can we get ashore?" asked Bryson, peering blindly into the light.

"Bloody water's gettin' on for a mile wide."

Brand was angry and his voice broke up as he began to cry. "We've come all this way. After all we've been through an' we're goin tae die on the ice. It's all your bloody fault Reilly. If you hadn't offered to go…"

"Now you just wait a minute! I never said anythin' about you or the others leavin' the ship."

"Ye knew we'd all be sent though."

"No we didn't," said Bryson. "We didn't say nothin' about ye."

"For God's sake, shut up!" shouted John. "Does it matter? We're here an' that's it. His eyes scoured the open water for signs of a boat; that proving fruitless he scanned the cliffs. He could make out some sheep on the crest of the cliff. "If we keep our eyes open we might see someone on land."

"Don't be stupid," said Reilly. "Who's goin' tae see us out here?"

Brand had stopped crying. "There are some smaller pans over there. Perhaps I could use one like a raft and paddle it ashore. Then I could get help." His conscience prompted him to add the last sentence.

"I think I'll do that too," said Reilly.

"What about me?" said Bryson. "I canna see at all now. Ye canna leave me here."

John was hardly aware that they were talking. He felt exhausted and was concentrating all his energies on scanning the clifftops.

"We'll get help," said Reilly.

"It's our only hope," added Brand.

"James, gi' us your stick, will ye? We could break it in two and use it for paddles."

"Bugger off. I might need it," replied Bryson, but before he could resist it was snatched from his hands by Brand.

"You rotten bastards! Ye wouldn't have done that if I could see. Give it back."

"Your rescue depends on us gettin' help, so I'm takin' the stick," said Brand. He broke it and gave half to Reilly.

Brand stepped carefully on to a piece of ice about five feet in diameter. This immediately tipped and he fell into the water.

"Barney," he gasped, swimming to the far side of the pan, "If I push this pan against the ice where you're standin' can ye put your foot on it – stop it tippin'?" At the second attempt this worked. Brand pulled himself up and laid across it. The pan supported his weight but was swamped. Carefully he moved into a kneeling position and began to push off other floes and work his way to the clear water.

John, in the meantime, was so intent on keeping his watch that he hardly noticed Brand go. Reilly saw a pan that was slightly larger than Brand's, but to get to it he had to cross to another pan first. The water between was about four feet wide.

"Move over Johnnie," he said, pushing the boy to one side. "I need to get a run up."

John moved a few yards towards the edge of the pan. Reilly ran across the floe and stamped hard on its edge to launch himself. As he did so the pan cracked, rocked and broke in two, John on one half and Bryson on the other. Reilly landed, slipped and fell heavily on to the other floe.

"Wha's goin' on?" asked Bryson staggering to keep his feet. John fell over and nearly went into the water.

The two parts began to drift away from one another. John hadn't the energy to rejoin Bryson on the larger piece, but seemed transfixed as the black gap widened. He returned to his watch.

Reilly had managed to climb on to his piece of ice fairly easily, and was now following Brand out into the clear water.

"Wha's happenin'?" asked Bryson. "Johnny, wha's happenin'? Are they away safely? Will they make it, d'ye reckon?"

Brand was out in clear water now, while Reilly was having difficulty in getting through the intervening floes. John couldn't tell whether Brand was making much forward progress but could see that he was slowly drifting sideways along the coast towards the open sea. He then realised that the ice on which he stood was also drifting in the same direction. In fact the gap between the land and the ice had widened a little.

"They're doin' fine," said John, wishing that he felt confident as he hoped he sounded.

"Davie Brand's out tae sea now, headin' for shore. Keep ye's fingers crossed, Jamie."

John continued his search of the cliffs. There was now a hint of yellow in the fading light on the cliffs. In an hour or two it would be dark.

Out of the corner of his eye he thought he saw a movement on the clifftop. A sheep? No. It was a woman. John nearly choked.

"Look! On the cliff... Someone's on the cliff! He screamed and waved. Bryson shouted and from the water John heard the other two call out and saw them wave. Their voices seemed so puny and the distance was so great. John screamed out for help until his throat hurt. With stiff fingers he removed his jacket and waved it like a flag, its white lining flashing in the waning sun.

John began to cry with the futility of the exercise. The woman paid no notice, but walked steadily away from the cliff edge, to be silhouetted against the sky. Her form shortened as she walked over the crest of the hill. He shouted again, and used his last ounce of energy to wave his coat in a final desperate attempt to attract her attention.

## 27. *The ordeal ends*

John's eyes began to water as he stared at the tiny figure on the clifftop. He wiped them and when he looked again could hardly believe what he saw. She was standing on the crest of the hill and was waving back. He blinked in disbelief. She was still waving.

"She's seen us! She's seen us!" As one, all the stowaways shouted and waved.

Reilly, who had found great difficulty in getting into the open sea on his small pan of ice now abandoned the attempt.

"What's happenin' now?" asked Bryson.

"She's hurryin' for help now," said John, "She keeps wavin'. The small figure in the long cloak rushed back along the path towards the house on the skyline.

John kept Bryson informed as to what was going on. "She's out o' sight now." His speech was becoming slurred.

It seemed a long time to those shivering on the ice, between her vanishing from view and a movement on the skyline indicating the arrival of several men. Again the stowaways shouted and waved. The men waved back and shouted something which was lost in the distance. Four of the men ran up the hill and out of sight over the skyline. The woman returned with a lamp and stood with the three men who remained. They occasionally waved the lamp and, as the evening closed in, this tiny lamp was the focus for the stowaways.

Brand, now about halfway to shore, still paddled his floe. He seemed further down in the water than when he had first set out, but nevertheless looked in control.

John's eyes were now sore. He could hardly bear to blink. He rubbed them and they watered continuously. His fingers had become increasingly difficult to move; they had curled into loose fists and were very blue and mottled. Another bout of violent shivering began. He felt as if he hadn't the energy for it and after a minute or so, much to his relief, it stopped again. The cold wind gusted and changed direction. The frozen cotton of his shirt touched the skin of his back. He wondered why he hadn't put his coat on again. The coat lay on the ice where he had dropped it. Frowning, he looked down at it, as if confused as to how it had come to be there.

A sudden shout from Reilly distracted him.

"They have a boat! They're coming to get us!"

Through sore eyes John focused on the figures on the cliff. They lowered a longboat down its rocky face. To the boys on the ice this seemed to take an eternity. When the boat was in the water, five men began their descent by rope.

"Wha's happenin' now Johnnie?" asked Bryson. John didn't answer but was still staring vacantly at his jacket.

He sank to his knees and then fell heavily onto his side, drawing his knees up to his chest.

"Johnnie?" said Bryson. There was no reply other than a groan.

"Johnnie!" Again there was no response.

"Johnnie, for the love of Christ, answer will ye." Bryson strained to hear even the slightest whisper but there was none.

"Johnnie, are ye there? Please... tell me ye's there... I canna see... I'm blind... I canna see nothin'. Where are ye? ... Johnnie!" Tears ran from his swollen, sightless eyes.

"I canna see..." he whined. Suddenly he felt a surge of panic "Help me! Help me... someone!" he screamed. His voice rattled out over the white expanse.

He pleaded: "Please God, if y' exist help me."

Between the sounds of his own sobbing he heard a distant voice. It was Reilly's. He had been trying to work his way back to John and Bryson. The Irishman was now just over fifty yards away, but was exhausted by his efforts.

"I'm over here," he said. He saw the small mound on the floe near Bryson. "Johnnie's laying on the ice. He's not movin'. I think he's had it." He looked around him and knew that he could never hope to cross the intervening distance to the boy without putting himself at risk in the dwindling light. He also knew that there would be little he could do to help him, assuming of course that he wasn't already dead.

"The boat's on its way, I can see the lamp," he shouted to Bryson. "It won't be long now. They'll see to him."

Brand's floe had melted rapidly in the currents and when the boat reached him he was swimming, using the stick to help his buoyancy. The boat then picked Reilly from the ice before coming to John's and Bryson's floes.

The strong hands of a fisherman reached out, grabbed John's ankle and pulled him into the boat. His body was stiff and he uttered no sound as he was wrapped in a warm woollen shirt and thick jacket, and laid in the bottom of the boat. The rescuer looked at his colleague, turned down the corners of his mouth and shook his head. Brand, quaking violently with cold despite his blankets, received the message too, and began to cry.

Bryson was offered an oar to guide him to the boat. The floe began to tip, but he was quickly pulled to safety.

Weaving their way through the floes to clear water was an arduous business and rowing from there to a point where the boat could be landed seemed to take an eternity. It was pitch black and they aimed for a pinprick of light in the distance. As this got closer, Reilly saw people waiting on the shore. They stamped away the cold and their breath was like clouds of smoke in the lamplight. He could see a cart too, with a horse.

For Reilly it was an unbelievably emotional moment when the boat's keel grated on the shore's gravel. Before long, the stowaways, with stiff and aching legs climbed into the cart. John, still motionless and swathed in blankets, was placed in the arms of a woman, who cuddled him to her, as if he was one of her own.

As the cart climbed the steep hill to the top of the cliff, Brand looked out into the blackness from where they had come and burst into tears. A farmhouse came into view. Neither Brand nor Reilly had ever seen such a welcome sight. The yellow light from the windows promised warmth that none of them had felt since leaving Greenock.

Bryson told the fishermen the story of how Hughie had died and McGinnes had refused to carry on. The men said that at first light they would take a party out to look for them. Brand said that he would go with them.

The cart creaked to a halt by the front door. John was quickly carried in and the rest followed. An open fire roared in the fireplace and there was an appetising aroma coming from a pot suspended above the flames. They gladly took a warm bath in the scullery. This began to thaw them. Brand, Bryson and Reilly were given clothes that had been warmed by the fire and wore blankets around their shoulders.

Gradually their shivering decreased as they became more comfortable, but as their hands and feet thawed out they fizzed painfully and it was a while before this subsided. The table was set and a steaming bowl of stew and chunks of soft bread laid out for each of them. All three of them ate enthusiastically.

John, meanwhile was not faring so well. Removing his clothes was difficult. He had drawn his legs up to his chest and had wrapped his arms around them. The two women who attended him found it hard to pull his arms away from his body and when they let go of them they sprang back to their former position. They dried his cold, white skin thoroughly and wrapped him in blankets, dressed the wounds on his feet and put him in a well-covered bed. When they had done all they could they stood back and looked at him. His extremities were still blue and he showed no signs of recovery.

"I think we're too late," said one of the women.

"Well, Martha, I'm not giving up on the wee lad yet," said Anna. "You take first shift 'til two, then I'll take over. He'll not die if I have anything to do wi' it."

At two o' clock Anna took over the watch. She was disappointed to see little change in John's condition. The other three stowaways were asleep, wrapped snugly in blankets on palliasses in the living room. Colour had returned to their faces and they looked at peace in the flickering glow of the fire.

She went up to John and stroked his cheek with her thumb.

"Come on little one. You've come this far, don't give up now." He still felt ice cold and she pulled the bedclothes up so that only a tuft of his hair could be seen.

It was still dark when a noise woke her. A high, tuneless voice was muttering the words of a cradle song:

> "*Oh hush thee my boy*
> *Oh hush thee my heart,*
> *Soon for dream's isle,*
> *Sleep's skiff will start.*
> *Oh, hush thee my baby*
> *Oh flower...*"

The words degenerated into mumbles. Anna looked at the boy's face. The blue coloration had gone. His nose, ears and cheeks were pink flushed. He muttered deliriously for a while longer before falling into a deep sleep.

At daybreak, the fishermen took the boat out to the ice. They traced the route back by following the bloody footprints made by John, but the ice was breaking up and the footprints suddenly ended at the edge of a floe. It became too dangerous to carry on with the search. In any case they were sure that McGinnes would not have survived the night.

The stowaways slept well into the morning. The first to wake was Reilly. He complained that he couldn't see and when Brand awoke he was suffering in the same way.

"Ah, we'll soon have ye right," said Anna, turning to one of her little daughters.

"Aggie, run down to Mary Mackay's house. Ask if she can spare us ten minutes." The little girl skipped out of the door.

"Will we be blind forever?" asked Brand.

"Bless ye no! We're used to this kind o' thing. We've got a remedy for most things." She removed Bryson's sock and dipped his foot into a bowl of oil.

"What's that?" he asked.

"Cod oil – marvellous for frostbite, have ye right as rain in no time." She took his foot from the bowl and massaged it. This gave him some pain, but he took it without complaint.

"How do that feel?" she asked.

"Hurts a bit."

"Aye well, it will for a while yet. Frostbite do take a bit o' care before it heals."

Later Mary Mackay came in carrying her newborn baby.

"Ah, ye've brought the wee mite tae see us." She scurried over to the proud mother and cooed at the rosy plump-faced child.

"I've a reason for callin' for ye, beyond seein' little Alexander," she whispered.

"Have ye fed him yet?"

"Aye"

"Good. I've a wee task for ye…" She led her into the scullery.

When she returned she sat Reilly in a chair with his head tilted back. Mary uncovered her breast and when Anna pulled open one of his eyelids she squeezed the breast, causing the milk to jet into his eye. She let the lid go and massaged the closed eye in circles.

"What was that?" asked Reilly.

"Oh, just somethin' to make ye better. Pay no mind to it."

Mary giggled, much to Reilly's discomfort. When both of his eyes had been done Brand and Bryson took their turn.

Anna went into the bedroom. John was still sleeping.

"Poor wee mite," she said.

The next day John regained consciousness, but it was a week before the swelling of his feet had gone down sufficiently for him to walk. One of the women made him some shoes of soft calf leather to wear while his feet healed.

Four months passed and John was settling into the local community. On one particularly warm day a group of men, women and boys were turning hay in a field which overlooked the bay.

John rested his hay fork, took off his straw hat and wiped the sweat from his brow. Strands of hay drifted in the breeze and small flies danced around him in the early September sun.

"What's up?" said George, a boy much his own age but a little taller.

"It's so hot. Just as well we've nearly finished. I'm starvin'."

"You're always starvin'. Maw says she thinks ye have worms."

"I have no such thing."

"I think she's only jokin'. She says ye have hollow legs too."

John carried on turning over the hay with his fork.

"I've always eaten well. In Greenock if ye didn't eat up quick someone else would grab it."

"D'ye really feel hungry?"

"Mmm."

"Shall we sneak a couple of apples from Jack Summers' orchard? It's on the way home."

"If ye like."

"One of us will have to keep a look out though. His house is nearby an' he's always about. You get a beatin' if he catches you. My friend Patrick kept him talkin' one time while I took tons of apples – he never found us out."

"My friend Hughie was a good stoolie too," said John, "we had all kinds of stuff. He could keep people busy for hours. I reckon he was the best stoolie in the world. He'd have loved it here."

John leaned on his fork and looked out across the shimmering sea. It was hard to believe that out there somewhere two friends had died. It all seemed so long ago. This was another world. Here the air was clean; people were kind and there was little poverty. When the cod were scarce, the cattle, sheep and crops gave an income. The work was hard, but they were healthy and happy.

George stopped working and pointed out to sea.

"That warship's still in out there," he said. "Been there since yesterday. I wonder why it's come? We don't see many ships like that around here."

John dug his fork into the hay and turned it over. A few strands flew away in the wind.

"Probably just visitin' or in for supplies." he said, "We used tae get all sorts in the docks in Greenock."

"Yeah, probably. Can't be any other reason, we ain't at war with anyone are we?"

"Not that I know of."

It was George's turn to wipe the sweat from his brow. He looked back up the hill at the other workers and was surprised to see a group of dust-stained, red coated soldiers, accompanied by two men in Naval uniform, coming over the hill and down the path. The officer went up to one of the workers who, after a brief discussion, pointed in John's direction.

"Come here boy," said the officer.

"Me?" asked John.

"Yes, you laddie. John stuck his hayfork in the ground and walked nervously up to the soldier who was laced liberally with bullion braiding.

"What's your name laddie?"

"John Paul, Sir."

"Would you like to go home?"

"I haven't finished work yet. They won't be expectin' me."

"No, I mean back to Greenock."

John was stunned by the suggestion.

"No Sir, I'm quite happy here thank you. I think I'd rather stay."

"Well, you can't stay. I have orders to send ye back to Greenock. Take him."

A soldier moved to either side of the boy, grasped him under the arm and marched him down the hill towards the shore.

"But Auntie Anna… and my things… Can't I go back tae the house first, tae say goodbye?"

"No time for that laddie."

As he was frog marched down the dusty path he looked back at the field workers. He saw George among them. He waved goodbye and began to cry.

*End*

# Epilogue

John was taken down to a jetty at Sandy Point, where a steam launch took him out to the warship, which was anchored in the bay.

Upon boarding the vessel he again met Bryson and Brand. All three stowaways were dressed in the garb of the Newfoundland fishermen: loose trousers, a long jumper and a hat made of dry grass. John was told that they were being taken back for the trial of the Captain and Mate of the Arran.

The stowaways learned that when it became known that two boys had died on the ice, the news rapidly spread among the fishermen and quickly came to the ears of the British Consul. It was two weeks before the Arran got free of the ice and when she arrived at Quebec, a consulate official boarded the ship and asked the Captain about the stowaways. He denied all knowledge of any stowaways, but some crew members told the officer the truth. The ship was immediately put under arrest and was moved from the quay out into the St Lawrence river and moored, with a guard mounted by police boats.

The ship was then ordered back to Scotland. The news of what had happened had preceded the Arran, no doubt embellished en route. No-one knew which of the stowaways had died. Some rumours said they were all dead. When she tied up at Albert Dock, a crowd of close to a thousand people lined the quayside, calling for the blood of both the Captain and the Mate. Ropes were slung from lampposts and the dock officials, afraid of what might happen, called in the police. It took the entire police force of Greenock to prevent the ship's officers from being taken by the mob.

After Kerr and Watt were arrested, the Procurator Fiscal of Greenock began to gather evidence, and after interviewing the crew sent the warship to find out what had happened to the survivors, if any, and to arrange for a ship to take them back to Greenock.

They were taken first to St Johns, where they waited for a suitable ship. While there, they were photographed and visited by hundreds of people, keen to hear their story. After an uneventful voyage of twelve days, the brig 'Hannah and Bennie' docked at the West Quay of Greenock on Thursday 1$^{st}$ October. Greeted by thousands of people, the boys were escorted to the Courthouse by twenty policemen, where John was joyfully reunited with his mother.

The trial opened in Edinburgh on November 23rd 1868. It lasted three days. Captain Robert Watt and Mate James Kerr were charged with assault, barbarous usage and culpable homicide. The charge of barbarous usage was dropped and after the three days, Watt was cleared of the charge of assault but convicted of culpable homicide. During the course of the trial, Kerr changed his plea to being guilty of assault only; this was accepted by the court.

The jury found both guilty as charged and Lord Justice Clerk Patton sentenced Captain Robert Watt to eighteen months imprisonment. The Mate James Kerr was given three months imprisonment. Both sentences were greeted with boos and hisses from the public gallery.

Commenting on the sentences, the Editor of the *Greenock Telegraph* wrote:

> "The punishment in each case appears very light, and those in court who had listened to the evidence heard the sentence in astonishment and greeted its delivery with hisses. Of course, the recommendations of the jury and the good character given both prisoners tended to mitigate the judgement, and it should also be borne in mind that the conduct of the accused, rough and unjustifiable as it was, did not proceed from any intention to bring about the fatal termination on which lay the main force of the whole case."

Nothing is known of what happened to Reilly. After working with a Newfoundland fishing fleet for a short while, he went to Halifax, Nova Scotia. He could not be found to bring back to Greenock for the trial.

James Bryson re-crossed the Atlantic to live with his parents, who had emigrated to New York. He became a streetcar conductor.

David Brand sailed to Australia and in Townsville, North Queensland, founded the engineering firm of Brand, Dryborough and Burns. He died suddenly in November 1897.

Peter Currie died of tuberculosis about two years after his return in the Arran.

John Paul followed his father into the shipyards and became a foreman riveter. He later moved his family to 30 Bridge Street in the village of Itchen, a suburb of Southampton, where he worked in the Wollston Ironworks. He died on 5th February 1913 and was buried in St Mary's Extra Cemetery. His grave has no markings.

Captain Robert Watt, after leaving prison, quickly returned to sea as Master but died in Pensacola, Florida two years later.

James Kerr, upon release, returned to sea as First Mate and later obtained his Masters' ticket. He sailed for many years as Ship's Master before retiring from the sea.